A Heart

Restored

Peacock Hill Romance Book One

Elizabeth Maddrey

Published in the United States of America by Elizabeth Maddrey
www.ElizabethMaddrey.com

Publisher's Note: This novel is a work of fiction. Names, characters, places, and incidents are either products of the author's imagination or used fictitiously. All characters are fictional, and any similarity to people living or dead is purely coincidental.

Other Books by Elizabeth Maddrey

Peacock Hill Romance Series
A Heart Restored
A Heart Reclaimed (Spring 2018)

Arcadia Valley Romance – Baxter Family Bakery Series
Loaves & Wishes (in *Romance Grows in Arcadia Valley*)
Muffins & Moonbeams
Cookies & Candlelight
Donuts & Daydreams

The 'Operation Romance' Series
Operation Mistletoe
Operation Valentine
Operation Fireworks
Operation Back-to-School

The 'Taste of Romance' Series
A Splash of Substance
A Pinch of Promise
A Dash of Daring
A Handful of Hope
A Tidbit of Trust

The 'Grant Us Grace' Series
Joint Venture
Wisdom to Know
Courage to Change
Serenity to Accept

The 'Remnants' Series:
Faith Departed
Hope Deferred
Love Defined

Stand alone novellas

Kinsale Kisses: An Irish Romance

For the most recent listing of all my books, please visit my website.

For my dad
For instilling in me a love of home improvement
and giving me the tools to make it a reality.

1

"You did *what?*"

Deidre McIntyre held the phone away from her ear as her best friend, Lisette, screeched. "I bought it. You should see it, Lis. It's amazing."

"I've seen it. Well, pictures of it. And 'amazing' leaves a lot open to interpretation. What on earth are you going to *do* with it?"

"Fix it up. Then, I guess we'll see." She had ideas. Lots of them. The problem was going to be figuring out which one to go with. But, given the state of the house—mansion, really—she had plenty of time to choose.

"You've lost your mind. What are you going to do out there in the mountains with no one nearby? What am *I* going to do without you?"

Now came the tricky part. Deidre cleared her throat. "You could always come help."

"Oh sure. I'll get right on that. Do you know me at all?"

"It'll be fun." Deidre put as much wheedle into her voice as she could manage, even though picturing her friend doing anything handy made her cringe. Lisette defined girly.

"Did you forget I hate dirt? No thanks. But if you actually get it renovated and want help with the interior design, I'm your girl."

That was the truth. No one did interiors like Lisette. "But just think...if you were here now, at the start of things, you could help *define* those interiors, as well as design them."

Lisette groaned. "You're evil. You know that's a dream of mine."

"And now it could come true. Come on, Lisette. You know you want to."

"I'll think about it. I do have a business to run. Clients who have contracts. That sort of thing? Seems to me you might have a few of those of your own?"

Deidre sighed. Business wasn't anywhere as good as it had been a year ago. Thus having time to scout out old houses and dream new dreams. "A couple, but nothing my sister can't handle."

"Claire's not there with you?"

"She didn't want to come." And she'd also been worried about their business. Since Deidre had taken over their dad's handyman service, they'd expanded and grown. Claire was determined to keep it from collapsing. "I'll get her here eventually."

"Uh huh. Look. Maybe I can swing down for the weekend. Maybe even make it a three or four day trip, but don't count on me for this."

"You sound like Claire." Deidre shook her head. "Neither of you think I'm going to finish this. I can hear it. Just you wait."

"You know we love you, right?" Lisette's voice held the tiniest hint of apology.

"Back atcha. So...this weekend?"

"Can't do it that fast. I'll let you know. Hey, I gotta run, I'm getting another call. Keep me posted."

Deidre ended the call and slipped her phone into the pocket of her jeans before backing up to view the front of her new...well, it wasn't a home yet. The house sat on fifty acres in the foothills of the Blue Ridge. Mountains rose in the distance to the west. Though she couldn't see it, the tiny town of Butler's End sat at the bottom of the hill the house perched on, and civilization wasn't too much farther down the road in either direction. But from here, she could've been in the middle of nowhere. This place was going to be something amazing. It had been, once, and it could be again, with a little bit of love and a whole lot of know-how. She happened to have both.

The front of the house needed to be cleaned. And several sections of the stone blocks that made up the facade repaired or replaced. She might have to hire that out. She dug out her phone and opened her note-taking app. She circled the house, tapping away as she saw things that needed attention. The landscaping, such as it was, would have to wait. The house was her first priority.

She rounded the corner, returning to the front of the house, and scowled at the dinged red pickup parked in the circular drive. She snapped a photo of the sign on the truck's door that featured an enormous cartoon frog wearing a straw hat and chewing on a piece of grass. There had to be someone who belonged to that heap.

"Aha." A man in jeans and a cream Henley that stretched over broad shoulders and well-defined arms jogged down her front steps and avoided the missing tread with ease that spoke of practice. "I heard someone bought the old girl. That you?"

Deidre kept her phone in her left hand, her finger hovering over the emergency number speed dial, and nodded.

"Pleasure to meet you, ma'am. I'm Jeremiah Crawford." He gestured to the truck and extended his hand. "I own Bullfrog Home Services."

Deidre took his hand, remembering her father's advice to have a firm grip and make eye contact. "Deidre McIntyre."

"Ms. McIntyre, I was just wondering what you planned to do with the place. She's been a fixture 'round here. A lot of the locals would be torn up if she got knocked down and turned into condos or something." He flashed a bright, toothy smile.

If the locals loved the place so much, why hadn't anyone taken better care of it? Sure, the previous owner was old and in a nursing facility now, but she had family. Family who'd seemed well pleased to be rid of the thing. "I have no plans to tear it down."

He cocked his head to the side. "Then what will you do?"

She crossed her arms. "I'm sorry, why do you care?"

"Well now, ma'am. If you plan to fix her up, I thought I'd offer my services." He dug in his pocket and produced a business card.

Deidre took the card and offered a tight smile. "I think I'll be fine. But thanks."

He nodded. "All right then. I'll leave you with that, in case you change your mind."

Deidre tucked the card into her pocket. She wasn't going to be able to do everything herself, but she'd planned to bring down some of her contractors from D.C. "I don't suppose you do stone work, Mr. Crawford?"

"Jeremiah. And, as it happens, I do."

"Have any references?"

"In the truck. Hang on a second." He crossed quickly to the vehicle and pulled open the door. Deidre caught a glimpse of a passenger foot-well littered with food wrappers. He took a binder off the seat and brought it back. "Here you go."

Lips pursed, she flipped through the pages. The photos were good. But you could edit images. "Any way I could visit some of these sites? Check them out?"

"Course. Why don't you give me a call in the morning and I can take you around?"

She opened her mouth to protest then shrugged. She'd find them faster if she was with him. And even if he was there glad-handing the client, she could see the work. It would speak for itself. "I'll do that."

Deidre rolled her sleeping bag out on top of the air mattress she'd spent the last twenty minutes inflating. There was an electric pump somewhere in the boxes she'd hauled in, but she couldn't find it. She'd unpack, in so far as that went, tomorrow. For now, her boxes were stacked against one wall in the room she'd chosen to be her bedroom-slash-office. She'd worry about furniture at some point. Maybe get Lisette to haul her desk and a real mattress down when she came. Or she could go up to D.C., raid the shed in her parents' back yard. It wasn't quite three hours up there, an easy enough day-trip if she needed it.

She already missed it.

Who knew there was no pizza delivery in the mountains? Didn't everyone have pizza delivery? And Internet. She could make do for a while turning her cell into a hotspot for her laptop, but when she had to deal with vendors online, she was going to need a better connection. Was there any chance she could talk the cable company into running a line up to the house? Or, better yet, fiber optics. She made a note to investigate it. Maybe when she was in town tomorrow.

Her cell rang and she grabbed for it, grinning when she saw her brother's smiling face on the screen.

"Hey, Duncan."

"Hey, yourself. How is it?"

Deidre dragged the air mattress over so she could keep her phone plugged in and still lay down. She stretched out and tucked an arm under her head. "It's a lot of work. But the house has so much potential. It's going to be amazing when it's done."

"Yeah?" There was a hint of skepticism in his voice. "And when's that going to be?"

She sighed, thinking through the list she'd made of what needed to be done. "There's a lot. A year? Maybe more. It'll depend on how much I do myself and how much I contract out."

He scoffed. "So we're leaning toward the 'maybe more' area?"

Her brother knew her too well. She hated to job stuff out. Especially work that mattered. And this place? It mattered. "You could come down and help. There's plenty of space. Heck, you could have a whole floor to yourself if you wanted."

Duncan hummed.

"Is that a yes?" There was no way. Duncan had his dream job as a landscape architect in downtown D.C. He'd worked years to get where he was.

"It's a maybe."

"What's going on? You love it at Marshall Brothers."

"It...might be past tense. They just hired a new partner instead of promoting from within, and I'm pretty sure he has someone in mind for my job."

She bristled. "They can't do that. You do amazing work. All your clients love you. They'd be fools—"

"Calm down. They're not going to fire me. But he's already taken two of my accounts in for review. I'm fairly sure he's going to decide I could have done something better and give them to someone else. Or put me on...I don't know, probation? Whatever it is, we're off to a rocky enough start that I've been brushing up my résumé."

"I'm sorry. That stinks."

She could almost hear him shrug. "I know God's got me. Honestly, I was praying about this and you came to mind. So I called."

"Ah."

"Don't give me that. I know you're struggling in your faith right now, Dee, but you know God works in our lives, right?"

She sighed. "Yeah, I do. I just..."

"Hey, I get it. But if I end up leaving, you'd let me come work with you?"

"Let you? Please. If you leave that job, you'd better get down here right away. I've got the fix-it skills, but when it comes to landscaping, I'll be making it up as I go along."

"Um. Don't do that. Just shoot me an email if you start thinking about tackling the gardens."

"Will do. Thanks, Duncan."

She hung up and rolled over.

God.

She and God hadn't been on speaking terms for close to a year now. Not since Paul.

With a mug of coffee in her hand, Deidre stepped into the observation tower and grinned. The view. There were no words. She could see all the way down to where the driveway met the main road that led into town. She turned and eyed the roof. That had to be one of the first jobs. It was between that and the windows. There was no point trying to renovate anything inside if every drop of spring rain worked its way into the house.

She dragged her phone out of her pocket and made a note. Would the local hardware store have cedar shake shingles? It was going to be easier to remove the entire thing and start fresh. Should she switch to asphalt? They had some nice looking shingles these days. No. Stick with the original. The whole point was to bring this beautiful girl back to life, not change her into something she wasn't.

Movement on the driveway caught her eye. He was prompt, there was no question. She tucked her phone back in her pocket, drained the last swallow of coffee from her mug, and turned to the stairs. Better to meet him out front than to have him poking around inside.

After a quick detour to the kitchen, such as it was, to set her mug in the sink, she grabbed her small purse and keys and was out the front doors, checking to make sure the latch caught, before he'd driven all the way up the hill.

His truck rattled into the circular drive, protesting as it came to a stop. He cut the engine and stepped out. "Mornin'."

Deidre licked her lips. No matter what else, the man looked good. "That it is. I thought I'd follow you down, I have some errands to run in town, and, depending, I might have to venture farther."

His frown disappeared almost as quickly as it appeared. "All right. You ready?"

She nodded and jingled her keys.

He got back in his truck as she crossed to her own. Would he notice she had her own handyman advertising on the door? Not likely. Men like Jeremiah— or Paul—saw a petite woman and automatically figured she was helpless.

Okay, so Jeremiah hadn't given off that vibe yet. But the day was young. She started the engine and lowered her window, waving for him to go ahead.

He was a courteous leader, she'd give him that. He hadn't run any yellow lights and always used his turn signal. But he drove like a little old lady, scrupulously five miles under the speed limit. She drummed her fingers on the steering wheel. What red-blooded man drove like that? He probably had his hands at ten and two o'clock, too.

Deidre eased up to the curb and parked behind Jeremiah's truck. He waited for her at the walkway leading up to a large stone-front home. She raised her eyebrows. It was gorgeous.

"Come on." Jeremiah waved her closer. "They're expecting us. We're a few minutes late. But I didn't want to go too fast."

She snorted. No chance of that.

"Yeah, well, you didn't get lost, did you?" He shook his head and turned, striding up the walkway.

Deidre cringed. She'd said it out loud. She hurried after him. "Sorry. One of these days I'm going to remember which one is my inside voice."

He scoffed and pushed the doorbell.

The door swung wide, revealing a distinguished older woman. "There you are, hon, why'd you ring the bell?"

"Mom, this is Deidre McIntyre. She bought Peacock Hill."

"Oh, it's about time someone bought that lovely old girl. What will you do with her?"

Deidre smiled. "Fix her up, to start. Then...we'll see. I understand Jeremiah's done some stonework for you? He said I could see it, as a reference?"

"Of course, of course. Come on in. Out back is the best place to see his work. Though there's pieces of him all throughout the house. He's been tinkering and fixing since he was big enough to hold a saw and screwdriver." Jeremiah's mother led the way past a lovely formal living room and into a homey kitchen. "Just out through the French doors there, Jeremiah can show you."

Jeremiah paused to kiss his mother's cheek before opening the door and gesturing for Deidre to go out. "The back of the house used to be all vinyl siding, but Mom and Dad wanted it to be consistent with the style of the house, so..."

"Wow." Deidre ran her fingers over the stone. It looked just like the front of the house. She studied Jeremiah. "You did this?"

He nodded. "Do you want to see another reference? I've done a few more in this neighborhood. Once they saw Mom and Dad's place, everyone decided the builders should have done it this way to start."

"No. This is...plenty." She took a few steps back and examined the back of the house. It really was lovely work, and she'd worked with some amazing craftsmen in D.C. "How busy are you?"

He shrugged. "I have enough work to make a living, but not so much I can't take on a new project."

"Okay. I'll be in touch when I figure out the reno schedule. If you're available, I'd like you to do the stonework on the facade. I could probably handle it, or I've got guys in D.C. I could call down to help, but..."

He cocked his head to the side. "You're not doing the renovations yourself, are you? This isn't something an amateur should take on."

"I agree. Which is why I'm handling it myself." Deidre dug in her back pocket, pulled out a card, and offered it to him.

His eyes widened. "I've heard of these guys. You work for them?"

She glared. "I am them."

2

Jeremiah sipped his lemonade and frowned at his parents' back yard.

"Was she impressed?" His mother pulled out one of the chairs at the table on the patio and sat, rubbing her arms. "Still a little chilly in the evenings. Spring isn't here yet. Not completely."

"She wants me to help with the stonework repair. So, I guess so. But she's no slouch." He pushed the card across the table.

"This is the group you wanted to work with. You never did say why you decided not to go."

Jeremiah hunched his shoulders. He still wasn't ready to talk about it. He'd been foolish to think Elise would welcome him tagging along. He saw that now. At the time, he'd thought they were in love. That they'd be moving to D.C. with a plan to marry sooner than later. Last he heard, she was dating one of the executives at the news station where she worked—someone who could provide more status than a carpenter-slash-handyman. Even if he was a darn good one of those. "I like it here, Ma. Can we leave it at that?"

"Sure. Working up on Peacock Hill though, that's a dream come true."

He nodded. He'd been saving up to buy it himself. But he was a year, possibly two, away from that reality. And now. Well, at least he could make sure the stonework got done right. "She didn't say what she planned to do after she fixed it up."

His mom laid her hand on his. "Maybe it'll be something nice."

"Sure. I guess. I just hate to see it become a private home when it has such a rich history. People should get to see it." If she kept any of the original character, at least. There weren't many Gilded Age mansions in Virginia. Even if this was just a summer home. It was a part of history that needed to be kept alive. He surged to his feet. "Anyway. Mulling it over isn't going to get the bills paid. I need to stop by Mrs. Anderson's and make sure her sink is still draining. Thanks for letting me stop by."

"You know you're welcome here anytime." His mom stood and wrapped him in her arms. "You also know I want grandchildren someday, right?"

"Yeah, I got that. Kinda need to find a wife first. And so far, I haven't figured out which aisle they're using for those in the hardware store."

"Well, as long as you're looking."

With a laugh, Jeremiah kissed his mom's cheek and strode toward his truck, his thoughts straying to the petite and lovely Deidre McIntyre.

"Let me help you with that." Jeremiah reached for the box that teetered on a high shelf and lifted it down to the flatbed cart in the aisle.

"I had it." The woman huffed and turned, nearly bumping into his chest. "Oh. It's you."

Jeremiah blinked before grinning. "Hi there."

She frowned. "Thanks. But I had it."

Was it worth arguing with the woman? The box had clearly been headed for the floor, despite the fact she'd had two fingertips on it. "Okay. Well. Sorry to intrude then. I'll just be going."

Jeremiah lifted a hand and turned, heading down the aisle to get to the back of the store where they hid all the plumbing supplies. He'd been after them to rearrange for years, but so far, no dice. If the big chain hardware stores did something one way, Al was determined that his store was going to be the opposite. Even if it meant huge quantities of roofing supplies were front and center for the three people who cared about finding them, and the plumbing supplies that every Saturday-handyman needed were tucked away in a back corner. But Al was here in town. The closest chain store was a twenty-minute drive away. And at this point, Jeremiah knew where everything was anyway. Roofing.

Was she really going to fix that roof herself? The one time he'd managed to get inside Peacock Hill, which hadn't been a strictly legal undertaking, the twelve-foot ceilings had seemed impossibly high. Three stories of those...she'd be over forty feet up. He shivered. No thank you.

He rummaged through the pipes and grabbed what he'd need to fix Mrs. Anderson's sink. Again. Maybe he'd swing by the roofing...no. She didn't want his help. She'd made that clear. Which was too bad, 'cause if it wasn't for her personality, she'd be exactly the kind of woman he was searching for.

Jeremiah swung into the tile section. His kitchen needed help. Most of his house did. It was a perfect example of what happened to a house from the 50s when it was updated by inept homeowners in the late 70s and left vacant in the mid-90s. But it had good bones and a lot of land. Plus, it kept him busy when work was slow.

Glass tile might be interesting. He paused and considered the options.

"Don't. Just...don't."

He turned, eyebrows raised. Deidre's flatbed was loaded higher than was strictly safe. How was she pulling that? Her arms must have serious definition. He flicked his gaze down, but a bulky sweater precluded any confirmation of that supposition. "Why not?"

"You're a bachelor, right?"

He nodded.

"And glass tile, particularly with the electric blue underlay, screams that from the rooftops. Particularly if you're putting it in your kitchen."

His mouth fell open. "How did you know I was thinking about my kitchen?"

Deidre shrugged. "I've done too many kitchen renos for men. They all start out wanting glass tile. My designer spends hours convincing them to consider something that won't be dated before the grout is dry."

"How many listen?" The tile was cool. Modern. Would it be dated that fast? Maybe.

"About half. The half that don't are good repeat business when they settle down and their wife gets a hold of the kitchen."

He snickered. "All right. What do you suggest?" ,

"That's not really my thing. But I can get you my designer's contact info. She's coming down soon. She could probably squeeze in a consult."

"Come on. What would you choose for your kitchen?" He gestured to the wall of offerings. "There has to be something here."

Blowing out a breath, Deidre took two steps and touched a marble mosaic. "Kitchen backsplash? This. It's pretty, but not so much that it overwhelms."

"Hm. I guess I could see that. Probably not with the countertops I'm making, but if you went with a traditional granite, that would be nice."

Her eyes lit with interest. "What are your countertops going to be?"

"Concrete. They're already finished, just need to cure a little more before installation." He could hardly wait. They looked good. Better than he'd hoped, given that he'd followed directions culled from various blogs and DIY websites.

"You should wait until they're installed before you tile. You'll want to match the finish—did you color them?"

Jeremiah nodded and pulled his phone out of his pocket. He swiped through his pictures 'til he found the photo he'd texted his mom. "This is the underside, but you get the idea."

"Ooh." She glanced up, her gaze locking with his. "You made those? By yourself?"

"So it seems." He put away his phone and sighed. No tile today. She was right. He should wait until the counters were in. But he was itching for a project he could knock out in a day. Nothing else in his house was going to offer instant satisfaction. Unless he decided to paint. But choosing a paint color was worse than deciding on tile. And what was wrong with plain white, anyway? "Thanks for the help."

Jeremiah tossed Danny a soda from the cooler and propped his feet on the deck railing.

"I still can't believe you're going to be working up at Peacock. Or that someone bought the place. How long has it been sitting on the market, six years?" Danny popped the tab and took a long drink.

"Five. Empty longer than that."

Danny snorted. "Remember when we broke in? I thought it'd be creepy. But it's really nice inside. Think the new owner's going to keep any of it?"

"Hard to say. She's not much on talking. Not about herself at least." Jeremiah frowned. She'd go on and on about tile choices though. Still, she'd been right. When he'd inspected the countertops currently curing in his garage, it had been clear that glass tile wouldn't be the look he wanted. Neither would the mosaic. He'd have to wait and see.

"Dude."

"What?" Jeremiah glanced at his friend.

"You spaced out. I asked if you thought you'd get any of the renovation work."

Jeremiah shrugged. "I took her over to my folks' house to see the stonework I did. She seemed to be impressed. I guess we'll see. She had a cart loaded up with roofing supplies when I saw her at Al's. Turns out he wasn't crazy for stocking all the cedar shingles. I'm pretty sure she bought every last one."

"Well I know you're not volunteering to help with the roof."

"She looks like she can handle it."

Danny tapped a finger on the side of his soda can. "Ugly then? Mannish?"

Jeremiah shook his head. "Nah. She's cute. Pretty, even. Tiny though. I don't think she's more than five two. Probably weighs a whole hundred pounds on a good day. It's hard to imagine she's the muscle behind D-Constructs."

"Seriously?"

"No lie."

"Did we know that was a girl?"

Jeremiah shook his head. Not that it mattered. It didn't. His mom could swing a hammer about as well as his dad. But it had been a shock to discover the owner of his dream job looked a lot like a famous cartoon fairy.

3

Deidre set down the pitchfork and stretched her back. She'd been second guessing re-doing the whole roof since she started. There were pieces here and there that probably were fine, but when all was said and done, the right choice was a complete replacement. At least the local hardware was well-supplied. And then she'd run into Jeremiah. That man was...there was no good word. 'Exasperating' came close.

And hot.

She didn't have time for hot. Plus, he'd been serious about the glass tile. Maybe if he lived in some sort of glass and steel modern monstrosity he could get away with it. But she hadn't seen any houses out here that looked like that. And he loved Peacock Hill. That much was obvious from the way he talked about it. Which added another word: endearing.

She didn't have time for that, either.

Her neck popped as she rolled her head in a circle before bending to the monotonous task of prying up cedar shakes. She'd been at it for a couple of hours and figured she had another hour, maybe two, left before it was too dark to be up on the roof safely. She'd get the rest of it off with a full day tomorrow and, if she was lucky, get started on the new one the day after that. At least there was no rain in the forecast.

The crunch of tires on gravel drew her attention as she finished one long stretch. She gathered up a pile of shingles and heaved them over the side to the open-topped construction dumpster that had been delivered while she'd been out with Jeremiah that morning. It wasn't where she would have chosen to park it, but it worked. And since she'd had no idea they were coming today, she wasn't going to be choosy. Even if she had to remind herself of that every time she saw the thing.

She grabbed her tools and lowered them to the ground with the pulley system she'd rigged, then descended the ladder.

"Are you insane?" Lisette slammed the door of her shiny silver coupe and stood with her hands on her hips. "Isn't roofing a two-person job?"

"I don't have two people. It's perfectly safe. I know what I'm doing." Deidre cocked her head to one side. "But I thought you had clients and couldn't possibly come down."

Her friend lifted one shoulder. "I don't have to meet with them in person again for another week or two.

I can make design presentations anywhere I have a computer. And I had a niggling feeling you'd be doing something stupid, so I came down here to save you from yourself."

Deidre shook her head. "I've been up on a roof alone before. And will be again. It's part of the job. But it's nice that you're offering to help. I hope you brought better shoes than those."

Lisette glanced down at her footwear. "I..."

Deidre smirked. "Kidding. Come on, I'll give you the grand tour."

Clicking the lock button on her key fob, Lisette wobbled across the gravel to the paved part of the driveway. "You're going to pave this whole thing, right? Down to the road? Maybe stamped concrete, that'd be pretty."

And cost a mint. She'd been mulling the options, but for now the gravel was fine. In the winter...well, she might wish for paving then, but that was a long way off. "We'll see."

Lisette stopped next to Deidre and stared at the house in front of her. "It's...something."

Deidre nodded, ignoring her friend's lack of enthusiasm. It got her every time she looked. The stone steps that led to a colonnaded porch. The matching square towers on either side of the house. And the floor-to-ceiling windows on the main floor that, given a little TLC, would once again double as additional entrances to the entertaining spaces. "Isn't it? I found a guy who can do the stonework. Once I get her reroofed and the cosmetics outside taken care of, she'll be a beauty."

"I guess. It's better inside, right? It has to be."

Deidre pushed open the front door and waved Lisette inside. She was either going to love it or hate it. There was never any in-between. After a brief mental debate, Deidre bet on hate. It wasn't shiny and sleek. Nor was it shabby chic. And those were the only two decorating styles her friend used. "Well?"

"That staircase."

It was the first thing you saw when you walked in. Three times the width of a normal staircase, it rose half the height of the high-ceilinged room to a landing where you could turn and finish ascending on either side. Above the landing was an enormous stained glass window depicting Peacock Hill in its glory days, complete with a flock of its namesakes parading their tail feathers for unseen hens. Miraculously, that was the one window that hadn't been broken.

Lisette climbed to the landing and reached up, touching the glass. She turned back with a frown. "You're going to take this out, right?"

"No. It's amazing. Why would I..." Deidre shook her head. "Just no."

"It's not safe. Think about it. They used real *lead* in this stuff back then. All of this," Lisette gestured expansively, "is a death trap. There's probably asbestos and who knows what. Honestly, Deidre. Can't you sell it and just come home?"

Deidre crossed to the stairs and sat, patting the space next to her. "What's going on, Lis?"

Shoulders slumping, Lisette moved to sit beside Deidre. She slipped her cell phone from her purse, swiped a few times, and offered it to Deidre.

Frowning, Deidre took the phone. As she read, her blood began to boil. "He dumped you in a *text*? What are we, twelve?"

Lisette shrugged, her eyes glistening. "I thought he was the one, with a capital O."

"Men are pigs." Deidre slung her arm around her friend's shoulders and squeezed. "Come on, let's go into town and get some dinner. And ice cream."

"We drove all that way for this?" Lisette frowned at the glowing chili pepper on the sign of the chain restaurant.

"Look, we're kind of in the middle of nowhere here. So yes, I drove to the closest big town to find something I knew you'd be okay with. I haven't tried either of the two places available in what passes for a town at the bottom of the hill on which my new house sits." Deidre yanked open the door and strode in. It wasn't like this was her idea of awesome either. But it was what they had available unless they wanted to drive an hour the other direction to Charlottesville. And the house more than made up for it. She held up two fingers for the hostess and glanced around. Didn't look like they were doing a bustling business on Tuesday night.

Lisette flopped into the booth across from Deidre and scowled at the menu. "So how long are you stuck down here?"

"I'm not sure." This probably wasn't the time to mention she wasn't planning to go back north. Sure, maybe the options were limited down here when it came to eating out, but there were benefits, too. All the land. No traffic. It was the perfect place for a getaway. She couldn't be the only one who thought so...which meant she had something to offer, a way to make a living that didn't involve swinging a hammer.

"What's that mean? You're not thinking of *staying* down here? What about your business? And...this? Come *on*, D. Aren't you going to miss being able to zip into D.C. whenever you want? There's so much to do at home. A big night out doesn't involve fake Tex Mex." Lisette leaned forward, her expression earnest. "Please tell me you're not serious."

Deidre rubbed the back of her neck. "Don't you get tired of all the hustle? There's never any quiet. Last night I lay in my bed and there was nothing. No cars. No sirens. I think I slept better than I have in years."

"You actually like it here." Lisette seemed to collapse in on herself. "You're staying."

"I think I might. Yeah."

"You've lost your mind." Lisette huffed out a breath. "What are you going to do with yourself?"

Deidre smiled at the server who appeared at the table with waters, rattled off a disinterested greeting, and took their orders.

"Spill it." Lisette unrolled her silverware and pinned Deidre with her gaze.

So much for getting out of that explanation. She took a long drink. "I was thinking maybe a B&B or weddings. Maybe both."

Lisette laughed. "Be serious. What's your plan?"

Deidre bristled. "Why can't that be my plan?"

"Because most people want frills and fripperies at their wedding and you're the biggest tomboy I've ever met. Do you even own a dress?"

"I have some skirts. What does that even have to do with anything?"

"If you don't know, I can't explain it to you other than to ask you to consider what it is most people wear to weddings. Hint: it's not jeans."

Deidre shrugged. "Okay, so maybe not weddings. People come down here to hike and sightsee. A B&B is better than a motel. Maybe in time, it could expand to a full-out resort. Add on a spa...what?"

Lisette laughed so hard she choked on her water. "I agree those are good ideas for the property. But, Dee, you're...you. You're a handyman. It's what you love. Why would you walk away from that?"

Why *would* she walk away from that? Even though her friend had decided to head back home after dinner, Lisette's words haunted her. Deidre flopped over in her sleeping bag and stared up at the ceiling. Because she needed a change. She'd been fixing other people's stuff for ten years, since her dad hired her at sixteen. He'd sold her the business when she turned twenty-one. Now she was twenty-six and the only time guys her age called her was when their plumbing was backed up or their fiancée wanted to change something in the house before they got married.

She didn't even get to go out on calls anymore unless she pulled rank. She was busy in the office managing the fifteen work crews that made up the company. Business was good. Maybe not as good as it had been two years ago, but she should be grateful. Instead, she'd run away. Maybe that wasn't completely accurate. Paul had made it hard to stay. He'd certainly been the reason she'd come down and found Peacock Hill six weeks ago. Her decision to buy had been impetuous. But she stood by it. She could run D-Constructs from here, if it came to that. Live here. Run the company from here. Maybe even open a satellite office. People down here needed handymen just like they did in D.C.

But she wanted more. She couldn't explain it. She'd tried. No one understood.

4

Jeremiah ran a solid bead of caulk along the top of the cabinets he'd built to make an island for his kitchen. They were simple, dark-stained oak. He hadn't decided on drawer pulls yet. He needed something plain, but not standard. Which might not exist. It certainly didn't at Al's. But that was a problem for another day. He set the caulk aside and rubbed his hands together. The concrete countertops were heavy. He should be able to lift them himself, but he probably should have asked Danny to come over and help. Saturdays were tricky. And now that the countertops were ready, Jeremiah wanted to get them in.

With help from a hand cart and some ropes, he got the island countertop in from the garage and lined up with the cabinets. After a deep breath, he hefted one edge up, then the other, and hurried to adjust it to the right position. Smiling, he walked around, scrutinizing each edge. It looked good. Just like he'd pictured when he'd first considered concrete counters. And it didn't help him envision a tile backsplash at all. Maybe when he got the rest in.

He reached for the caulk gun, stopping when his phone rang. The number was from out of area. He was used to getting calls from numbers he didn't know, that was the down side of using your cell phone for business and personal use. Might as well answer it. He was going to need help to do the rest of the counter anyway.

"Jeremiah Crawford."

"Hi. It's Deidre. McIntyre? I was calling to check on your schedule next week, see if you were available to do some work? I'm trying to get the outside fixed up before I tackle things inside. Which probably doesn't matter to you."

She was a phone rambler. He wouldn't have guessed that. Jeremiah leaned against the cabinets. "I'm pretty clear. What did you have in mind?"

"Any chance you could come by this afternoon and I can walk you through it? I'd like to get an estimate—time and cost—before we go further."

"I can do that. Are you free afterward? I'm setting my countertops today, thought you might enjoy seeing them." And maybe helping out. He'd wait to mention that part.

Deidre's sigh crackled in his ear. "I'd like that. I'm probably heading over to Waynesboro for dinner anyway. Y'all need a fast food place or two in town."

He chuckled. "If you can convince one to come, I'll frequent them. The cafe on Main isn't bad, if you're in the mood for soup and a sandwich. But I've never been a fan of Sinclair's. It's more bar than anything. Though my friend swears by their nachos."

"I like nachos."

"I'll keep that in mind." He winced. "I...what time do you want me?"

"Whenever. I'm putting new glass in the broken windows, so I'm here."

"All right. I'll see you in a bit." Jeremiah ended the call and set the phone down. He crossed to the fridge and considered the contents. He could make nachos. Danny said Jeremiah's were better than the ones at Sinclair's. Grabbing a bag of chips at the grocery store on his way up to Peacock Hill wouldn't take him much out of his way. And then, if it seemed reasonable, he'd offer to fix supper. It wouldn't be like a date. He found her attractive, sure. He had a pulse. But even the little bit of time he'd been around her, yeah, she wasn't the kind of woman he wanted for himself. He wanted someone like his mom. A woman who enjoyed staying home, wanted kids, someone who'd fix him supper after a long day, that's what he wanted. Deidre wasn't any of that. And there was nothing wrong with that, it was her choice. And no one could fault her. She'd made her company an incredible success. Honestly, he'd still like to work for an outfit like that someday, if he ever got out of Podunk.

He scoffed. Like that would ever happen. He'd had a chance and God had made it pretty clear that he was supposed to stay put. Nothing had changed on that front. Thus, the house. If he was going to be stuck there, it was time to settle down, make it his home.

Jeremiah shook his head and pushed himself off the cabinets. Might as well wash up and go to Peacock Hill, find out what's what. And if Deidre stayed for nachos, well, then he'd get a chance to eat with a woman who'd done something he admired. Maybe he could pick her brain, get a few pointers.

Jeremiah stepped out of the truck and fought to keep his jaw from dropping. The woman worked fast. She'd only been in town a week, and yet she'd managed to replace the roof and the glass in all the windows he could see from the front of the house. Following the sound of hammering, he headed left. She was up on a ladder, working on a window for the third floor. How was she doing all this by herself?

He waited until she started climbing down before speaking. "It's looking great."

Deidre jolted, clutching the ladder. She blew out a breath and smiled as she stepped to the ground. "Thanks. Maybe don't sneak up on people on ladders."

"Sorry. I thought you saw me."

She tugged her phone from her jeans. "You're quick. Feel like helping with some of these windows? I have a system, but it's tricky and I've nearly dropped two panes. I'd just as soon not replace my replacements."

"Sure." Jeremiah shrugged. Windows were easier with two people. And it'd give him a chance to see what working with her was like. Maybe it'd be easier than he suspected. Besides, she'd owe him then, and have to help with the counters. "You want to go in and work from there? I don't mind ladders."

"Okay." She pointed to the broken window to the left of the one she'd just finished. "That's next."

Jeremiah watched her walk away. She had a brisk, no-nonsense stride, and for someone as short as she was, she covered the ground quickly. She filled out her jeans in all the right places, too. He shook his head and grabbed the ladder. She wasn't his type. Even if she was the most attractive woman he'd seen in...a long time. He'd leave it there.

He climbed the ladder and tugged on his work gloves. She'd already removed the broken glass from the frame. There was a wire brush on the floor by the window. He reached through and grabbed it. There were a few places that needed a bit of scrubbing to remove the old glazing putty.

Just slightly out of breath, Deidre strode into the room. "Thanks, that was next but I see you know what you're doing."

"I'm glad you're not putting in modern windows. Even if they'd potentially save on heating and cooling, they never look the same."

She nodded and held a rag to the mouth of a bottle. "That's what I thought."

"What's that?"

"Linseed oil. It conditions the wood and helps the new glazing adhere better." Deidre rubbed around the frame.

"Nice."

"Here. Go ahead and put down a line of putty."

They worked well together. She didn't micromanage, or order him around. She did what she needed to do and seemed to assume he'd do the same. He set the putty knife on top of the can. "All set."

Deidre nodded and reached for the pane of glass beside the window. She stripped off the brown paper and passed it through to him. "There are glazier's points and more putty in that bucket hanging from the top of the ladder."

Jeremiah followed her pointing finger. Clever girl. He slid the glass into place, shifting it so it had the right amount of space on each side and was settled into the rabbet groove like it needed to be. Deidre provided counter pressure from the other side, ensuring that it stayed where it needed to. Keeping one hand on the glass, he dipped his hand into the bucket for the small triangles that, placed around the edges of the glass, would keep it in position. He set them, then worked them into the wood frame with the tip of the putty knife he found in the improvised tool-holder as well.

"Looks good." Deidre gave him a thumbs-up from inside. "Go ahead and do the seal."

Jeremiah pulled off his work gloves and set them in the bucket before collecting a ball of the putty and rubbing it between his hands to form a long snake. When it was the right thickness, he worked it around the edges of the glass. Satisfied that it was good, he took the putty knife and smoothed it into a professional looking bevel.

"You did this by yourself? Isn't it usually a two-person job?"

She shrugged. "I get that a lot. But I can get the job done on my own. And sometimes that's what matters."

With quiet agreement, they moved on to the next. In just a little over an hour, they'd finished that side of the house.

"That's plenty. Thanks. I can do the rest. Let me show you the stone that needs repair." Deidre jerked her head toward the front of the house.

Jeremiah made his way around and met her on the front steps.

"You probably don't need me to point out the problem areas, but...I'm going to anyway."

He followed as she pointed to the various spots with damage. He showed her a few that she'd missed. It was good that she seemed to be interested in keeping the house as it was meant to be. She was fixing it up, not turning it into something it wasn't. Nothing she wanted done was beyond his ability. It was just going to be a matter of time. And finding the right materials.

They finished circling the house and ended back in front.

"What do you think?" Deidre tucked her hands in her pockets.

"All doable. I'll need to look into the materials, unless you've done that already?"

She shook her head. "It's on my list. But if you have suppliers already, I'm fine with that."

"I have some. I'll need a little time to draw up a quote. End of next week?"

"That'll work. Now, how about those countertops?"

He grinned. "Sounds good. Want to just ride down with me? That way you don't have to complain about how slow I drive when someone's following me."

"I was going to head out for dinner after..."

"I thought I could make some nachos. Break in the new counters."

"Are your nachos any good?"

"Why don't you tell me?"

"I can't get over the fact that these are the first ones you've made." Deidre ran her hand over the countertop. "They're incredible. The veining you did is tricky. I thought you said they were simple?"

"Well, compared to some of the ones you see online, they are. Anyway, there are some great tutorials out there. You ever watch that show with Paul, oh, what's his last name? Something Italian, I think. Anyway, it's kind of a goofy name, 'Flippin' for You.'"

Her face paled, but she nodded. "Rossi. It's Paul Rossi. I haven't watched it in a while though. Not a lot of time for TV."

"That's fair. This last season wasn't as good as the first two, but it's still interesting to watch. Either way, you should check out his website sometime. He has some great tutorials. The veining was one of his." Jeremiah patted the surface. "Anyway, why don't you make yourself at home, and I'll whip up the nachos."

"I'm expecting great things, just so you know. I take my nachos very seriously." Deidre hoisted herself up on the counter. "So maybe I'll just stay and watch."

He shook his head. She was adorable. Not that he was interested. Her personality wasn't exactly what he'd thought after their first meeting. Which was a positive bonus. But still. Not looking. Even if his mom did want grandkids. Deidre didn't strike him as someone who wanted to be a mom. "You're just going to sit there."

"I can chop, if you want, though I kind of feel like I already paid for my supper since I helped you install these babies."

"Nah." He opened the fridge and started pulling out ingredients. "Just watch and be amazed."

She chuckled.

It wasn't long until he was sliding his biggest tray, covered in chips, meat, beans, and cheese into the oven. "That's the trick, right there. You have to melt the cheese in the oven. It keeps the chips crisp and blends all the flavors. Microwave just makes things soggy. Then you add the tomatoes, olives, jalapeños, salsa, and sour cream when you serve them."

She sniffed. "Smells good. I'll give you that. Can I help set the table or something?"

"Sure." He opened a cabinet and took down two plates. "Silverware's in the last drawer. Napkins should be on the table. I think I have some soda in the fridge, otherwise we're stuck with water. Have a preference?"

"I'll grab a soda. Want one?"

Jeremiah slipped his hand into oven mitts and nodded. "Sure."

While Deidre set the table, he finished doctoring the nachos and carried them over. "Ta-da."

She nodded. "Impressive. I've seen worse at restaurants."

He laughed and pulled out her chair. "Well, hopefully they'll live up to your discerning tastes." Deidre gave him a weird look before she sat. Was he not supposed to hold her chair? His mother would skin him alive if she found out he didn't. Mentally shrugging it off, he took the chair next to hers and offered his hand. "Can I say grace?"

"Oh. Sure." She rested her finger tips on his.

Even with the tiny point of contact, electricity raced up his arm. Jeremiah ground his teeth together. She wasn't his type. Maybe if he repeated it to himself he'd finally get the message. He closed his hand around hers and bowed his head. "Thank You, Jesus, for the food we're about to eat, for keeping us safe on our various work projects today, and for giving us hearts, heads, and hands we can use for Your service. Amen."

"Amen." She pulled her hand out of his as if it was burned and reached for the spatula resting on the side of the tray of nachos. "Let's see how you did."

Jeremiah's hand was still tingling. Maybe it was some kind of sudden onset neuropathy. He reached for the utensil when she set it down. Huh. He could feel the spatula fine, so he hadn't pinched a nerve or anything. Scooping up a healthy portion of nachos for his plate, he glanced over at her. "Tell me how you got into construction."

5

Deidre slid a loaded chip in her mouth and chewed. The man could make nachos. And countertops. How had someone not snapped him up already? He even had that southern Virginia drawl that wasn't quite *southern* but was just a bit softer and gentler on the ears than the no-accent, too-busy-to-think Northern Virginia way of speaking. If she hadn't given up relationships completely, she might look into snagging him for herself. Her system was still buzzing from holding his hand for a prayer. *A prayer.* She and God weren't speaking right now, but she was pretty sure she wasn't supposed to get all tingly inside when someone was praying.

"It's a long story."

Jeremiah gestured to the nachos. "We have a lot of food. And I can make more."

She picked up another chip, dunking it into the pool of beans that was sliding off the pile of food on her plate. "Dad was a handyman growing up. He did well enough to support us, but the three of us—me, my brother, and my sister—all got jobs as soon as we could. I got one with him. Mom was annoyed. She wanted me to do something more ladylike, maybe sell clothes or something, but I wanted to be with Dad. He taught me everything he knew and, since college wasn't in the cards unless I took out a ton of loans or won the lottery, I worked for him while I took a few classes at the community college so I understood the business side of things. Then I got a few certifications and before I knew it, Dad wanted to step back from the business a bit and limit what he took on, so he offered to sell it to me. I took him up on it and...here I am."

"But the business is up north."

She sighed. "So I'm told. It's doing okay. They don't need me, honestly. My sister runs the office, all the crews. I was only there to fight through financial stuff and smooth any ruffled feathers. I can do that from here if I need to. I haven't had a chance to do any honest work in close to six months. And even then, it was only because I bullied my way onto the job. It feels good to get my hands dirty again."

"What will you do when you finish?" Jeremiah popped the top of his soda and took a long drink, his gaze never leaving hers.

That was the question, wasn't it? Lisette had shot down all her ideas. And she wasn't wrong. Not really. Deidre didn't have the skills to do any of the things she'd like to do with Peacock Hill. But she could learn them. "I don't know yet."

"No immediate plans to sell?"

She shook her head. That was one thing she wasn't doing. "No. Not if I can avoid it. It's a beautiful house. It needs to have people in it."

He smiled and something caught in her chest. "It's good you see that. Get that. I wondered."

She'd always had a feel for houses. It was one reason she'd wanted to work with her dad, so she'd know how to take care of them when she found a gem. "I don't believe in flipping houses just because you can make a good profit. When you invest that kind of time, you need to know it's going to be enjoyed by someone for a long time to come."

"You don't think people who buy flips enjoy them?"

Deidre shrugged. "Maybe they do, maybe they don't. The point is, you don't know. Don't you want to know?"

"I do. But I've also been told that's unusual." He reached for another helping of nachos. "It's nice to know I'm in good company."

Warmth spread through her but she frowned. She wasn't going there. Even if he was good looking. "What about you?"

"What about me?"

"How'd you end up a handyman?"

He shrugged. "I've always been good with my hands. Started fixing things here and there, word got around, people would call. Before I realized what was happening, I had a business. I thought about leaving—heading up your way, actually. Thought I'd try to get on one of your crews. But ended up staying put."

Something—sorrow?—flashed in his eyes. Would he talk about it? "What happened? From what I've seen, you would've been a shoe-in."

Jeremiah shrugged. "The girl I'd been dating since our junior year in high school was moving up there. She had a job with one of the local TV stations. I figured I'd go along, and, once we both were settled in a job, I'd propose, we'd get married, and, I don't know, live happily ever after, I guess."

"That sounds...perfect. Why aren't you busy working on your two-point-five kids?"

"Turned out that she didn't want me to tag along. The move was her way of breaking up without having to bother with the messy part of telling me she didn't love me. Never had." He stood and started collecting plates. "It's not as tragic as it sounds. I like it here well enough. And for now, this seems to be where God has me planted. So, I choose to bloom."

How could he be so content after something like that? "Why don't you blame God?"

He set the dishes in the sink and turned. "Why would I?"

"Wasn't that your dream? Marrying her, living up near D.C.? And He took it away."

Jeremiah frowned. "God didn't take it away; Elise did. It's not as if God owes us the fulfillment of our dreams, even if they're dreams He gives us. I think sometimes God gives us dreams to see if we're willing to trust Him with them."

Deidre pushed her laptop aside and rubbed her neck. She checked the time and reached for her phone, tapping the speed dial for her brother.

"D? You okay?"

"Hi Duncan. Yeah, I'm fine. Is it too late? It's too late. I can talk to you tomorrow."

"It's fine. I'm still awake. What's up?"

"Someone—a friend—said something tonight that got me thinking. I wanted to run it by you." Jeremiah was a friend. The more she thought about it, the truer it seemed. Even if she'd only had a few interactions with him.

"Friend, huh? I'm glad you're making friends already. What'd she say?"

"He. Doesn't matter. Anyway. Do you trust God with your dreams?"

"Like at bedtime?"

She laughed. "No. Your dreams. Goals. Aspirations. Like this job issue you're having. You said God's got you. But...you also said you thought He gave you that job. How can He give you a dream and then yank it away?"

"Ah. I guess it comes down to what your end goal really is."

Deidre frowned. "What do you mean?"

"My end goal isn't this job—or any job, really. I want God to use me where He thinks I'll be most effective, doing whatever it is He wants me to do. I think, given that I have an aptitude for landscape architecture, that's always going to be part of it. But if it isn't, that's okay too."

"Where'd you come up with that? Mom and Dad were big on using our brains, our talents, having goals, and doing what it took to achieve them. Where does God come into that?"

"That's tougher. I've been where you are, Dee, thinking God only mattered at the front part, where He gave us a brain and sent us out into the world to do our best with it. But He doesn't walk away and leave you to figure it out on your own. If you're willing to ask Him for help, and really listen for His guidance, He's going to show you where He wants you to be."

Would He? When Paul had approached her with the offer to help out in his flipping business, it had seemed like the exact answer to her prayers. The handyman business had been floundering. Working with

Paul got them jobs and contacts for the future. A lot of their repeat business still came from that, even if Paul wasn't part of the picture anymore. But the way Paul left—the damage he'd done to her reputation with the production company after their first season filming—how was that God?

"You're quiet. Did I make you mad?" Duncan's voice was soft.

"No. Just thinking. Thanks."

"Don't mention it. While you're thinking, ask yourself this: why are you down there with that big old house to renovate? Were you following God's nudge or running away?"

Deidre bristled. "I'm not running from anything."

"Okay. One more piece of advice?"

"Sure, why not."

"Find a church. You'll hear God more clearly if you're working on your relationship with Him."

Deidre smoothed her hand over the single skirt she'd thrown in her suitcase at the last minute. Her mother always harped on the fact that ladies needed to have something nice just in case. Looked like listening had, finally, paid off. Even if God didn't care what she wore. And she was obsessing about this entirely too much.

Church. It had been a long time. At least two years. Maybe a little longer? She'd spent ten minutes on the Internet on her phone trying to figure out where to go. For such a rural area, there were plenty of options. She sifted through the papers on kitchen counter. There it was. She grabbed Jeremiah's business card—she really ought to just enter him in her phone. She opened a new contact, tapped in Jeremiah's information and saved it, then opened a new text.

"Hi. It's Deidre. Can I conga crutch with news?"

When she saw how it sent, she groaned and tapped again, this time more carefully.

"Come to church with you."

When she was sure nothing had been weirdly corrected, she hit send. She could almost hear him laughing at her.

"Conga crutching sounds like fun but I usually avoid news. Church good 2. Want me 2 pick u up?"

Did she? Then she'd be stuck with him, on his time table. But it beat wandering the winding roads looking for something while the service was about to start.

"k. am ridiculous."

With a sigh, she sent a correction.

"Ready"

This is why she didn't text. Ever. But she hadn't been able to bring herself to call. What if he'd thought she was hitting on him? Or if he hadn't wanted her to come? Those awkward pauses when someone was trying to figure out how to let you down gently? No thank you. At least texting saved her from that. Sort of.

":) will leave soon. C U in 15ish"

Fifteen minutes. She pressed a hand to her stomach. What was she thinking? She was thinking maybe her brother was right. Not that she'd tell him that. Church. *All right, God. Maybe it's time I came back?*

6

Fifteen minutes. Jeremiah glanced down at his jeans and, frowning, stalked back into his bedroom. He had some khakis in the closet. They were probably even ironed. He peeled off the Henley he'd chosen and dug through a drawer for a polo. There was enough spring in the air that he could justify short sleeves. Shoes. No. He drew the line at his shoes. His work boots were comfortable and decent enough. Most people couldn't even tell they were boots, because his pants covered...what was he doing? Shoes. For crying out loud, he might as well dig up a purse to carry.

He tucked his shirt into the dress pants, ran a hand over his hair, and stuffed his wallet and phone into his pockets. Grabbing his keys off the kitchen island, he headed out to the truck. He was half-way down the driveway when he stopped.

"Dang it." Jeremiah threw the truck into park and jogged back inside to grab his Bible. The woman was driving him to distraction. He'd barely slept all night, replaying their conversation over and over, looking for any hint that she felt the attraction he did. He'd given it up as hopeless.

And then she'd texted.

He chuckled. Clearly she didn't re-read things before she sent them. Which fit. She didn't strike him as someone who took time on things she deemed unimportant. If it mattered, sure, she'd focus and get it right. That was obvious just looking at the repairs she'd already made to Peacock Hill.

He turned up the long driveway that wound up the mountain to the mansion. Would she pave it? A couple of winters here and she might just realize she needed to. Would she stay through the winter? A pang hit his heart. He wanted her to. He'd have to see what he could do about that.

He shifted the truck into park and cut off the engine. Deidre started down the steps as he rounded the hood. Was she ever going to let him get to the door? He opened the car and waited. "Morning."

"Hi." She stopped at the truck and held his gaze. "Thanks for picking me up. I...you could've just sent me directions. Or an address. I have GPS. Or..."

Jeremiah shook his head and pressed a finger to her lips. "It's my pleasure. You look lovely."

Red washed over her cheeks and she looked away before running a hand down her navy blue skirt covered with tiny white flowers. "Is it too much? Am I over-dressed?"

"No. You're lovely. You'll see a range of clothes. Hop in."

"I should've worn jeans, right? You were gonna wear jeans." She slid into the truck, holding her purse on her lap.

"I was. But when I knew I was picking you up, I changed." Jeremiah winked and shut the door. He kicked himself as he went around to the driver's side. He was coming on too strong. And she wasn't his type.

But he wanted her to be.

"I'm so glad you came today." Jeremiah's mom wrapped Deidre in a hug and wiggled her eyebrows at Jeremiah. "Can you join us for lunch?"

"Oh. I...don't want to intrude."

"Nonsense. You remember the way to the house?"

Deidre shot Jeremiah a look.

He shrugged. If his mom wanted Deidre to come for lunch, he wasn't going to object. All through the service, he'd been trying to figure out how to ask. So much that he'd only caught the very first scripture reference. He was going to have to listen to it online when they got it up later in the week. "I picked her up."

His mother's eyebrows shot up, and a smile spread across her features. "Even better. I'll find your daddy, Jeremiah, and see you two in a little bit."

"Are you sure..." Deidre twisted her fingers together.

"It's just lunch. My mom likes to do a big Sunday meal. She's always inviting someone." He winced. Way to make her feel welcome. "I didn't mean—"

"No, that helps, actually. You're sure it's not an imposition?"

Jeremiah took her hand, forcing his thoughts away from the shivers that caused. "I'm sure. Come on, you should at least get a chance to meet the pastor on your way out."

Deidre didn't pull her hand away. Did she feel it too?

"Hi, thanks for coming this morning." The pastor smiled as he shook Deidre's hand. "Friend of Jeremiah's?"

"Oh, well, yes. I guess?" She stared up at him, looking lost.

"Deidre's new to the area. She bought Peacock Hill and is fixing it up. And I'd like to think we're friends, yes." He squeezed her hand. Her fingers tightened around his.

"Well, now, I can't wait to see it when you get it finished. That house is a bit of a family member to just about everyone who lives in the area. It was a real shame when old Mrs. Ebbit had to move into the nursing facility over in Charlottesville. Her kin never did seem to know what to do with the place. I'm glad they found someone to give it the love it needs. Hope we'll see you back again with us."

Deidre nodded.

Jeremiah led her out into the parking lot. "You okay?"

"Why is everyone so nice?"

He cocked his head to the side. "You say that like it's a bad thing."

She hunched her shoulders. "It's not. But I keep looking for the thorn in all these roses."

"Oh, we have thorns, plenty of 'em. Give it another week, maybe two, and the gossip will start trickling to your ears. Mrs. Patterson over there, don't look, she's the worst about it. She'll tell the whole town about something and then smile to your face and ask how you're doing."

"What'd she say about you?"

He frowned. "What makes you think—"

"Please. The way you said her name gave it away. Come on. 'Fess up."

Jeremiah opened the passenger door of his truck and helped her in. He had no intention of answering that question. Not one. Maybe she'd let it go. He closed the door and rounded the hood. "I should call Mom and see if we need to pick anything up on the way."

"First answer the question."

He dropped his phone in the cup holder and shifted in his seat so he could look at her. "You're not letting it go, are you?"

"Nope. Like a dog with a bone, when I want to be." She smiled and batted her eyelashes at him.

He sighed. "Fine. In high school, I snuck out of the house—only once, mind you—but she caught a glimpse of me and, before I knew what hit me, everyone knew about it. Just my luck that the youth pastor's house got egged that night."

"You egged your youth pastor's house?" Deidre shook her head. "I'm surprised they still let you in the front door of the church."

"I did no such thing." He started the truck and backed out of the parking space. "And she never said I did, either. She just hinted at it." His voice went up several octaves. "Oh, isn't it so sad? That Jeremiah was such a promising young man, but he's out at all hours doing who knows what. Why just the other night I happened to see him..."

Deidre snorted out a laugh. Her hand flew to her face.

"Did you just snort?"

She shook her head. And snorted again.

Jeremiah laughed. "Well, well. Just wait 'til Mrs. Patterson finds out about that."

As he turned in at Deidre's driveway, Jeremiah looked over. "I'm glad you texted me this morning. Thanks for staying to lunch."

"Even though I didn't really have a choice, I'm glad, too." She grinned.

"Maybe we could do it again next week?" He felt her eyes on him but kept his gaze firmly on the road ahead.

"Okay. But maybe you could come for lunch here, instead?"

"You cook?"

"Not like your mom, but you won't starve."

It wasn't a ringing endorsement, but he'd risk food poisoning for more time alone with her. "It's a date."

She cleared her throat.

Jeremiah pulled up behind a white van with "Flippin' for You!" emblazoned on the side across pictures of the host and some of his projects. "Um."

"He wouldn't." Deidre threw open the door before the truck was completely stopped and jumped down. "Paul!"

The girl could bellow. Jeremiah shifted into park and cut the engine, hopping out of the truck and tucking his hands in his pockets. He followed in Deidre's wake as she headed around the side of the house, still yelling for the host. Jeremiah reviewed what she'd said about the show when she was over yesterday. She'd sidestepped. Neatly. And she'd known the guy's last name. Which suggested...he stopped as the TV host, looking camera-ready in his khakis and denim shirt, sleeves rolled up to his elbows, grinned and scooped Deidre off her feet to turn her in a circle.

"Put me down, Paul." Deidre pushed at his chest.

Paul set her down and landed a smacking kiss on her cheek. "You've done it again, Dee. I don't know how you always find these houses. Who's the client?"

Deidre crossed her arms. "Why?"

Jeremiah leaned against the corner of the house, his mind racing. She didn't look like she'd welcomed the kiss, but there was something there. A history. He shook his head. What was it with him and women who wanted to be on TV? Was he ever going to find someone who'd be content with him? Even if it meant they never moved away from here?

"Don't be like that, Dee. This house *needs* to be on my show. Just point me to the homeowner..." Paul trailed off as his gaze found Jeremiah. His grin had the TV sparkle and used car salesman built in. He crossed the grass with his hand out. "That must be you. I'm Paul Rossi, it's great to meet you."

"Jeremiah Crawford." He took Paul's hand. There was no way that man did any work with tools. Unless he coated his hands with petroleum jelly and wrapped them in socks every night like his grandma used to do. The image made him smile. "I've always enjoyed your show."

Deidre cleared her throat as she closed the distance. "Paul."

"Don't worry, Dee. This way you're not even responsible for me finding out. Convenient, right? Of course, that might mean you don't get in on the crew. We'll have to see." Paul turned his attention back to Jeremiah. "Now, Mr. Crawford, how about we head inside and you can give me the tour and I can tell you what being on Flippin' for You can do for your property."

Jeremiah shook his head, his gaze darting to Deidre. "I don't think so. You see, there appears to have been a misunderstanding. As much as I'd love to own Peacock Hill, I was about a year away from having the cash. So, this beauty belongs to Ms. McIntyre, and I believe I'll be going. It was a pleasure."

"Jeremiah!"

He kept walking. Jeremiah wasn't interested in being caught in the middle of old friends. Or more than friends. That put a sour taste in his mouth. He couldn't compete with someone like Paul Rossi. Didn't want to. Except. He yanked open the door to his truck, his gaze falling on Deidre as she hurried around the corner of the house.

"Please wait, Jeremiah."

He sighed and stood with one foot in the truck while she scurried the rest of the way. "I really do need to go. I can probably get that quote together for you tonight so you have it when you start figuring out your production schedule."

"It's not like that. I don't know why he's here. I'm not flipping this house." She rested her fingers on his hand. "Please believe me."

He held her gaze, his heartbeat thundering in his ears. "I want to. But it's a little hard to ignore this. And him." Jeremiah jerked his head toward Paul who was headed their way, his hundred watt smile still on full. "I'll get you that quote. Let me know if you decide to go that route."

7

Deidre's shoulders fell as Jeremiah drove off. She spun and drilled her finger into Paul's chest. "Why are you here?"

Paul stepped back, his smile dimming. "Come on, babe."

"Don't call me that." She hissed through her teeth and shook her head. "You know what? I don't care why you're here. Get off my property."

Paul leaned against his van. "There's no way you bought this place. Just tell me who the client is. You and I both know they're not going to turn me down. And a place like this? It could really help my ratings."

"I care about your ratings why?" She waited a beat. "Oh, that's right. I don't. Get off my property before I call the cops."

He fell into step beside her as she went up the front steps. He'd always been persistent. Why had she ever found it charming? On the top step, she paused and turned around. "You can go down to the county record office and verify it for yourself, but I own this house. And I'm just not interested in having your pathetic show associated with it. I want to renovate in a way that honors the history of this building, with good quality workmanship. Not the slap dash work your new crew does, which, if you recall, is why I left the show in the first place."

"And as part of leaving, you agreed not to flip houses." Paul nodded to the front door. "So why don't you let me in and we'll discuss what we're going to do."

"No chance. I'm not flipping this house. I live here. And I plan to continue to do that." The sureness of that statement struck her. This was home now. She hadn't been fully committed before, but now? It was right. What did that mean for D-Constructs?

"Please. You're not going to stay out here in the boondocks. The nearest real town is what, a thirty, forty-minute drive? With the highlight of having two popular chain restaurants? You know you're going to miss D.C. So cut the charade, and let's get down to business." He reached for the door.

Deidre slapped a hand on his chest. "I'm not sure what's so hard for you to understand about the word no, but I'm going to say it one more time. No. If you're still here in thirty seconds, I'm calling the cops. Twenty-nine."

She continued to count as he held her gaze. When she hit fifteen and took her phone out of her pocket he shook his head and started down the steps toward the van.

"You'll be hearing from the show's lawyer."

Let them call. She hadn't violated any of their agreements, which was one of the reasons she'd had the time to look around for a house like this. The way the final agreement was phrased, it hadn't been clear that D-Constructs could be hired by folks flipping a house, so Deidre had erred on the side of caution. It had cost her three crews. Business was still fine. There was more than enough work, even without flipping, but flipping had the potential for big money and they'd had a good reputation.

Until Paul had gotten a hold of it.

"How did he even know where I was?" Deidre paced across the foyer, cell phone clamped to her ear. She studied the molding around the ceiling. That would need some touch up. Shouldn't be too hard, but was it wood or plaster? "You still there?"

Lisette cleared her throat. "I, uh, might have mentioned it."

"What? Why would you do that? Why were you even talking to him?" Little spots danced in front of her eyes and Deidre took a deep breath before reminding herself that there was no point in yelling.

"He misses you. He never wanted things to end the way they did. I just think you're too hard on him."

Deidre stopped and sat on the bottom stair, her stomach tightening into a knot. "You've been talking to him all along. For the last year."

The silence on the line said it all.

"Look. We were friends, too. It's not fair for you to expect everyone who was friends with Paul, or involved in the show, to walk away just because you did."

Deidre pulled her hair back into a ponytail and wrapped the hair band she kept on her wrist around it, pretending the hair was her so-called-friend's neck. "You're designing for him."

"We're talking about it. It's been a year. And at the end of the day, I could use the boost it gave to my business." Lisette blew out a breath. "I'm sorry you found out this way. I'd planned to say something."

"Oh, sure. Since it's only been twelve months. I can see how you simply haven't had time." Deidre glared across the foyer and ground her teeth together.

"I haven't had the words. I knew you'd react this way."

"You think? My best friend is still friends and—apparently—business partners with the man who broke my heart and damaged my business, and I'm supposed to be okay with it? You know what? Just take Peacock Hill off your priority list. 'Cause I'm pretty sure I can figure out paint colors and furniture on my own. And when

Paul screws you over, don't come crying to me." Deidre hit end on her phone and lowered her head to her knees.

If God really cared about her, He had a weird way of showing it.

8

Danny tossed Jeremiah a soda. "You're still heading to church tonight, right?"

He popped the top and took a long drink. "Yeah. I just need to send this quote off to Ms. McIntyre and then I'll be ready. You grabbing a ride with me?"

"If you don't mind. Then you could drop me at the garage? Matt thought he should be done with my car by then." Danny flipped a chair around and straddled it. "What happened?"

Jeremiah tossed a look at his friend and turned back to his computer. "What do you mean?"

"Weren't you calling her Denise on Sunday?"

"Deidre." He sighed, rubbed his neck, and hit save.

"Denise. Deidre. Whatever. It starts with a D. I repeat the question: what happened?"

Jeremiah shifted to look at his friend. "I'm not exactly sure. When I dropped her off after lunch at Mom and Dad's, Paul Rossi was there."

"From the house show?" Danny's eyebrows shot up. "Nice. Are they going to do Peacock Hill? That'd be cool."

"Sounded like that's what he wanted. But she wasn't having any of it. And...it was pretty clear there was a history there." And he couldn't compete with that.

"History? But not current events?"

Jeremiah shrugged. Sure, it hadn't looked like she was excited to see Paul. She certainly hadn't thrown herself into his arms. But how much of that was because Jeremiah was there? No way to know.

"So...what? You just skulked off with your tail between your legs?" Danny shook his head. "Dude. You've *got* to get over Elise."

"I have. I just don't see the point in signing up for Elise, part two. Seriously, man, you've watched the show. What exactly do I have that Paul Rossi doesn't?"

"From what I saw on Sunday? Deidre."

Danny's words echoed in his head all through youth group. Thankfully he wasn't in charge of anything spiritually important this week. He'd ended the night by giving his group of boys their assignment for the week, slapping a ton of high fives, and chatting briefly with one overly concerned mom who didn't seem to get the fact that boys—especially high school boys—were going to clam up every now and then. And that was okay. It didn't mean they didn't love their mom, or that they were doing drugs, or anything bad. It just meant the kid was processing something and chances were good, that if she left him alone for a little, he'd come to her eventually. At least, that's how it'd always worked for him.

Maybe his mom was just really cool.

"Ready?" Danny lounged against the side of Jeremiah's car.

"Yeah. You figure Matt's still there? We're about twenty minutes later than usual. Sorry."

"Yep. Just texted him to be sure. He's doing some paperwork while he waits." After Jeremiah clicked the fob to unlock the doors, Danny tugged open the door of the truck and hopped in. "Appreciate the ride."

"Easy enough." Jeremiah started the truck and backed out of the now-empty lot. "What are you doing this weekend? Any plans?"

Danny shook his head. "Why?"

"Thought I might go camping. Wanna come?"

"Don't you have work you should be doing?"

Jeremiah frowned. The only potential work he had in the hopper was up at Peacock Hill. The other odds and ends that kept him afloat were during the work week. And sure, now that spring was hitting, he'd be getting a lot busier. People liked to spruce up their houses once the snow was gone; power wash the decks, that sort of thing. But he wasn't reduced to working weekends just yet. "Nope. So, are you in?"

"You need to call her."

"Why?"

"Because it's ridiculous to go camping when you could be working up at Peacock Hill and making headway with the most eligible bachelorette to hit our town since Missy James moved here in the seventh grade."

Jeremiah laughed. Missy James. Now there was a memory. "I'd forgotten all about her. She was here what, three years?"

"About that, yeah. And had every guy in the class—and most of the guys in the classes above and below—trying to catch her eye. Then it comes out that she's not allowed to date 'til she's a senior."

"So Matt says. Did anyone other than him verify that with her? I still think it was Matt saving face after she shot him down."

It was Danny's turn to chuckle. "I dare you to say that to his face."

"No way. I'm not stupid. He can still take me." Jeremiah pulled to a stop in front of Matt's garage. "Here you go, curbside service with a smile."

"I missed the smile, but then, I avoid looking at you whenever I can. Never have been into horror."

"Jerk. Get out of my truck." Jeremiah grinned and punched Danny on the arm. "So that's a no for this weekend, right?"

Danny paused with his hand on the truck door. "Tell you what, you call and actually talk to her, and, if you're not otherwise engaged after that, then yeah, sure. I'll go camping. But I'm inviting Matt, too, so the two of us can gang up on you until you're done moping about Elise."

"I'm not moping."

"Uh-huh. Sure. So, deal?" Danny cocked his head to the side.

Jeremiah frowned. "Fine. But only because I hate camping alone."

Jeremiah started the dishwasher and swiped a sponge over the counter. Clean enough. He checked the time on the microwave and frowned. Still only nine. Which meant he could call. Probably. Maybe he'd text. It was basically the same thing. And then if she was asleep, it was less likely to wake her.

He thumbed open a new message.

"Hey. U get my proposal?"

There. He'd made contact. He could let Danny know to pick up marshmallows when he packed for the camping trip. Carrying his phone with him on the off chance she got back to him, he flopped into his recliner and clicked on the TV. His phone buzzed with a new message.

"Yes. Imhotep to have a starting date for U by frier."

Jeremiah frowned at the text message, trying to decipher it.

"So it looked good?"

He waited. After a minute, his phone rang.

"This is ridiculous. Please, if we're any kind of friends, don't make me text. I'm not sure why my phone has Egyptian Pharaohs in the autocorrect. Nor do I understand why it would think I meant that instead of 'I'm hoping' squished together because I didn't hit the space hard enough."

"Are we any kind of friends?" Jeremiah winced, mentally pulled the words back into his mouth, and swallowed them. "Never mind. Back to the proposal."

"No. It's okay. I—yes. I'm hoping we are. I'd like us to be."

"Okay." He cleared his throat. Better to let it go at that than to get into everything else. "So the proposal looked good?"

"It did. Thanks. Are you sure we're good?"

"Why wouldn't we be?"

Deidre sighed. "Because Paul is a jerk and probably gave you the very wrong idea when he came—uninvited, I'm going to add—on Sunday."

"It's not really my place..."

"Oh, please. I'm not an idiot. You think I didn't notice that you disappeared?"

Jeremiah sighed. "It's fine. It's none of my business. I just wanted to give you space. It seemed like you and Paul had some stuff to sort out."

She groaned. "No. We didn't. Look. That show— Paul's show? It was supposed to be mine. Or his and mine. And then, next thing I knew, it was his show and I was in the background doing all the work. After that, they were hiring cheaper workers and I was out and contractually barred from flipping houses, because they don't want anyone to know that Paul's incapable of hammering a nail in straight, let alone any of the more complex work they do on the show."

"Seriously?" It was hard to believe. Paul was in every scene, getting things started off.

"Yep. Those shots of him demo-ing a wall or installing a cabinet? They're set up beforehand, meticulously, so all he has to do is hit a pencil mark with the sledge hammer or finish tightening down a screw the last two turns. And even then, it usually takes three or more tries. He thinks I'm flipping Peacock Hill. I'm not. I wasn't kidding when I told you I have ideas—that I'm staying. I just can't seem to get anyone to take me seriously."

The sincerity in her voice rang true. On all of it. But one question still niggled at the back of his mind. He might hate himself later, but he had to ask. "This is probably none of my business...but were you and Paul together?"

"You're right. It isn't. But yeah, we were. Right up until I realized that he only wanted to be with me because I was good at home repair. So I ended things. And he wasn't willing to keep working with me. Since his was the face of the show, it was pretty clear who had to go. But that's how I ended up with the money to buy this place. And, given how steadily D-Construct's business has been falling off since then? Having the means to start fresh is a blessing."

"God's got a way of cushioning our falls, doesn't He?" Jeremiah smiled. "We still on for church Sunday?"

"Yeah. If you're sure."

"I am. Any plans on Saturday?"

"Not really."

"Want some?" His heart hammered in his chest. Was he really asking her out? Even if it meant competing with Paul Rossi?

"You know what? I really do."

9

Deidre tugged open the door and blinked. "Claire? What are you doing here?"

"I can't do it anymore, D. I'm sorry. I figured I should tell you in person. Can I come in?"

"Of course." Deidre stepped back and let her sister in. "Do you have a suitcase in the car? I can go grab it."

"I'll get it later." Claire dragged a hand through her hair as she surveyed the house. "This is gorgeous. No wonder you snapped it up."

"I knew you'd love it if you saw it." She rubbed her sister's arm. "I'm glad you came down. Now, tell me what you meant. What can't you do anymore?"

"Is there somewhere we can sit?"

She didn't have much in the way of furniture yet. The room she was using for sleeping and as an office was...spartan. "I have some stools in the kitchen."

Deidre crossed the wide foyer and pushed open the door that led to the kitchen. The room had been updated in the late fifties—probably moved from the basement level where it was originally situated. At least they'd stuck to a black and white color scheme instead of making it all pink or teal. The appliances themselves were in decent enough shape that she was going to try and keep them. It added a little something to the space. She'd stuck a small, pub-height table in one corner.

"This is nice. More modern than the rest but, in this case, that's a bonus. It's functional?" Claire ran her hand over the stove as she passed it.

Deidre nodded. "You want a drink? I have some sodas in the fridge, or I can make tea?"

"I'll grab a soda. Want one?"

"Sure." She hopped onto a stool and propped her elbows on the table. "What's going on?"

Claire popped the tab on her soda and set the other can in front of Deidre. "We lost two more crews today. We're basically down to the guys who subbed for Dad when he was running things. The restrictions on what kinds of jobs we're allowed to do, courtesy of the legal vultures from that stupid show, make it hard for the guys to get enough work. If they're officially on our payroll, then the restrictions apply to their freelance jobs as well. I don't know what we should do, but I can't make all the decisions on my own."

"I never expected you to." Deidre laid her hand on her sister's. "I'm sorry you thought I did. Maybe...this is God's way of saying it's time to close down."

Her sister raised her eyebrows. "There are two things in that statement that leave me speechless."

"All evidence to the contrary."

"You're a riot. But seriously. Are you talking to God again? 'Cause that would be an answer to my own prayers."

Deidre sighed. "I'm not sure I ever stopped. Not completely. I just...why does He let people like Paul prosper when those of us who do the right thing have to flounder around? Don't answer. I don't think there is an answer, not really."

"What happened?"

"I went to church with the guy who's going to start on the stone work here next week. The sermon was from Habakkuk. I mean really, who preaches from Habakkuk? But it was all about trusting God in the midst of disaster—and how you can ask all those questions, but you still have to trust." Deidre shrugged. "It got me thinking."

"I'm glad." Claire smiled. "And the closing thing? You're really thinking about that?"

"Yeah. This place is special. I want to fix it up, but then I want to see it thrive. I want to be here for that. And okay, maybe I don't know everything I need to know about running a bed and breakfast, but I can learn. I'll go back to school, if that's what it takes."

"Bed and breakfast?" Claire tapped her lip with a finger. "I'm not sure this place screams B and B. But...what about conferences and retreats? And weddings?"

Deidre's grin faded as Lisette's scorn echoed in her ears. "You don't think that's ridiculous?"

"Nope. Maybe I'm wrong and the space isn't suited. Give me the tour and we'll put our heads together. If you're serious about staying here and closing D-Constructs? I'll come down and pitch in. The only part I'm struggling with is managing a losing battle."

"I can't promise that's not what this'll turn into."

Claire nodded. "I know. But right now, I'd say this has a lot more promise than D-Constructs."

Deidre's shoulders slumped. She'd known it. But hearing it out loud was a different story. "Let's take that tour, then I guess I'm calling Dad."

"Do you mind if my sister tags along?" Clad in jeans and a t-shirt, a windbreaker tied around her waist, Deidre pulled the door open wider. "Come on in."

Jeremiah stared at her for a second before stepping in and looking around. "It hasn't changed much in the last ten years. I was worried the wood on the walls or the floors would get water damage. Anyone could see that old roof needed to go."

"Yeah. It got me twenty grand off the asking price. And an unhappy seller, but what did he expect? You let a house fall apart, you're not going to be able to sell it for top dollar. So. My sister?"

"Oh. Yeah, of course. The more the merrier, right?" He tucked his hands in the back pockets of his jeans and leaned, gazing into the formal dining room.

Deidre laughed. "Claire's gonna be at least fifteen more minutes. You want the nickel tour?"

He grinned, nodding. "I really do. But first let me call Danny and see if he wants to tag along. We could pick him up on our way. He loves to hike the falls."

She gave him a long, appraising look. Had inviting her sister been a bad idea? It wasn't like this was a date. Was it? Oh, man. Had Jeremiah wanted it to be? She wasn't used to decoding signals anymore—had gotten out of the habit after Paul. There probably had been some she missed, but that made it easier to keep everything firmly in the friend zone anyway. Was he interested in her that way? The thought made her warm inside and did quivery things to her middle. And she'd just invited her sister along on their first date. Typical. "Danny?"

Jeremiah covered the bottom of his phone with his hand. "Best friend since high school. He's great, you'll like him. Oh, hey man. You still free? Uh-huh. No...no...we're gonna hike to Jones Run Falls, maybe stretch it to Doyle's? Her sister's tagging along...'course. Ok. Pick you up in maybe thirty?"

"He's in?"

Jeremiah nodded, dug a coin out of his pocket, and tossed it to her. "Let's have that tour."

He had a thousand ideas and most of them were good. A lot were the same as what she'd put together in her plan, or close to it with a few tweaks that might be an improvement. She'd made a few notes as they talked and would think about it. He had a good eye and an appreciation for the house that was palpable.

Did he like her because of Peacock Hill?

Deidre shifted and caught Claire's eye in the back of the extended cab truck.

Claire made an exaggerated face and sighed. "Are we there yet?"

Jeremiah laughed. "Just about. The parking area is up ahead soon. I promise. You two okay back there?"

"Remind me to meet you there, next time I agree to go hiking with you. They didn't have guys over six feet tall in mind when they designed back seats for trucks." Danny's knees pressed into Deidre's back as he moved.

"I'm sorry. You can sit up front on the way home. I think I've got this as far forward as it can go. And I don't need the leg room."

"You're the only one, D." Claire crossed her legs. "I'm not sure they had anyone over the age of ten in mind."

"Hey, now. Be kind to the truck, she's sensitive. And I think we'd all like her to take us home when we're done hiking, right?" Jeremiah patted the dashboard and crooned quietly. "It's okay, girl, they just don't appreciate you like I do."

"What is it with men and their cars?" Deidre shook her head. "Honestly, it's a machine that gets you from point A to point B. Not a person."

The truck's engine revved loudly.

"Ha ha. That was you. Machine. Inanimate. Not alive." Deidre glanced over her shoulder at her sister. "Right, Claire?"

"I'm...going to take the fifth. I don't want to walk home."

"Chicken. Danny?"

Danny held up his hands. "My SUV has a name and everything. She's not as finicky as this gal, but she still deserves respect."

Jeremiah snickered. "She's not finicky. She's prissy. Or do you wash her every week for your own benefit?"

"There is nothing wrong with keeping your ride clean and shiny. You could take some pointers, though I was pleased to see you shoveled the files out of here. Going to finally get some organization to your business?" Danny unhooked his seatbelt the moment Jeremiah cut the engine and pushed open his door. "Oh, yeah. Circulation."

Deidre rolled her eyes as she hopped down from the passenger seat. "Were you in theater in high school?"

"Sure." Danny flashed a grin. "But I always got the plucky comic relief roles. Never could hold a candle to Jeremiah."

He'd acted? She turned, taking in his lean, muscular form. Her mouth went dry. Yeah, he could pull off leading man.

Jeremiah smiled and whistled a few bars from The Music Man as he grabbed a backpack out of the truck bed and slung it over his shoulders. "Ready, troops?"

Danny and Claire both shrugged.

Deidre gave an absent nod, unable to reconcile her picture of Jeremiah as a down-to-earth handyman with the information that he'd had the lead in a musical. Even if it was several years ago that was...not what she would ever have pictured.

"What about you? Ever do any theater?" Jeremiah nudged her with his elbow as they started down the trail. Danny and Claire had fallen in behind them and were working through the standard getting-to-know-you chit chat.

"Just backstage stuff. Building sets and props, that kind of thing. When I had time. I worked a lot as soon as I was old enough. It's really pretty here."

He smiled. "Just wait 'til you see the falls."

10

Jeremiah could barely keep his smile under control. It was a gorgeous spring day and he was on one of his favorite hikes with the woman who'd captured his heart. Heart? Interest. He'd meant interest. They'd made it to the waterfall with relative ease. No one had complained about the pace he set, which was new. Danny could be a bit of a whiner if Jeremiah got into the groove and started going fast. Had he been slower than usual? Maybe. Deidre had interesting commentary and seemed to enjoy stopping to examine groups of mushrooms or lichens, anything that caught her eye.

The music of the water on the rocks was soothing.

"Now we have a decision. We can head back the way we came, or we can keep following the trail and loop around past another set of falls." Jeremiah tossed a stick into the water and watched as it floated away.

"What's the difference?" Claire sagged against a big rock. She didn't look like she got out into nature much.

"About four miles." Danny shook his head at Jeremiah. "We ought to just go back the same way. I'm not sure anyone is up for eight miles today, unless you've got snacks squirreled away in that backpack?"

He'd meant to bring something. But after he'd grabbed water, his mom had called and by the time he'd gotten off the phone, he'd been running late. "Nope. Sorry."

"Another time, maybe?" Deidre patted his knee. "I'd be interested in seeing more. It's lovely out here."

He nodded, tingles working their way up his leg from the brief contact. "All right. That's a deal. Ready to head back?"

Danny and Claire took the lead, and were several yards ahead before Jeremiah and Deidre had collected their water bottles and checked for debris. As they started down the trail, Deidre's foot caught on a rock and she tripped forward. Jeremiah caught her hand to help steady her.

"Thanks." She smiled up at him.

He squeezed her hand and was about to let go when her fingers threaded through his. The grin that split his face was probably goofy, but he didn't care.

Jeremiah climbed down the ladder and pulled off his gloves. How the Pattersons got so many leaves in their gutters over the winter continued to mystify him. He was here every fall after their trees had dropped their leaves, and that should be enough. But, like clockwork, Mrs. Patterson was calling to complain about spring rain overflowing and pouring down the sides of their house. And there was certainly enough blocking the channel to the downspouts that it was worth getting up there.

"All finished?" Mrs. Patterson appeared on the front stoop with a tall glass of pale yellow liquid in her hands. "I brought you some lemonade. It's store bought, mind, so you won't hurt my feelings if you don't like it."

He took a long drink, fighting a wince at the tart yet overly sweet liquid. How did that happen? "It's refreshing, thanks. You should be all set now until the fall, but call me if it happens again."

"Oh, now, I'm sure it'll be just fine. Always is after you visit. Saw you with that northern girl at church again on Sunday. You serious?"

Jeremiah nearly choked on the swallow of lemonade. "No, ma'am. Deidre's new in town, I'm just being neighborly."

"Mmhmm. Don't think I'm so old that I don't know what *that* means. You be sure to make it official before you start living up at that big house with her. And none of that, oh what is it I'm always seeing on the Facebook? Netflix and chill, that's it. I know all about that, too. I made my nephew Matt explain it."

Poor Matt. "Sometimes it just means staying in and watching a movie, Mrs. Patterson."

She scoffed. "Jeremiah Crawford. Sin like that's been around since Adam and Eve. Mr. Patterson used to try and get me to go watch the sunset with him. But I knew just what he was after, same as any smart girl today. So just you be a gentleman. Though...I don't wonder if you couldn't do better than a snorter. Heard her laugh at something that other gal who was with her said, turned right into a pig snort. Sad state of affairs if a lady can't be bothered to keep her emotions under control."

"I'll keep that in mind, ma'am. That was probably her sister, Claire, who was down for a visit."

"I know that. I asked around. I didn't figure any of the women around here would make someone snort. Though perhaps she's just predisposed. What'd you say her name was? The northern gal?"

"Deidre. Deidre McIntyre."

Mrs. Patterson nodded. "Well, if she's doing justice to that big place up the hill, she can't be all bad. You make sure you get your mark on it too, though. No sense in having your wife make all the decisions on your home."

Wife? "You're getting a little ahead of..."

"Pshaw. I saw how you looked at her, boy. Same look that greets me every morning in the eyes of my own man. You're sweet on her. She might not know it yet." She pursed her lips and narrowed her eyes at him. "Maybe you don't even know it yet. Doesn't change what is. Now, how much do I owe you?"

Jeremiah took another long swallow of lemonade, draining the glass but doing nothing to moisten the desert in his mouth. "Same as the fall, forty even."

Mrs. Patterson held out a check, already filled in. Why did she ask, when she knew the answer?

He took the check and offered her the empty cup. "Thanks. Let me know if you need anything else done."

"You going to be doing lawns again this year?"

He nodded. It wasn't high on his list of things he wanted to do, but basic maintenance and repairs didn't pay the bills year round, and a good lawn care season kept a healthy balance in his bank account during the dry spells. "Yes, ma'am."

"Sign us on up. Mr. Patterson's getting too old to be out here in the summer heat."

"I'll mail you a contract. Thanks, Mrs. Patterson."

She smiled and patted his hand. "You're a good boy, Jeremiah."

He grinned as he headed for his truck. Mrs. Patterson could make him feel like a misbehaving teenager at the drop of a hat, but she could bolster his confidence just as easily.

He plugged his cell into the charger as he started up his truck. Just one more stop to make before his jobs for the day were done. As Mondays went, it wasn't horrible. If only he could think of a reason to casually swing by Peacock Hill and ask Deidre to dinner.

Settled in his recliner, Jeremiah clicked on the TV. Not that there was likely to be anything worth watching. But...he was too restless to read, and though there was always paperwork for the business...that didn't appeal either. He eyed his phone. Maybe he'd give Deidre a call. But why? He didn't have anything to say and they weren't quite at the 'just wanted to hear your voice' stage of their relationship. Even if that's exactly where he was. Text. He'd text. Then, if she was busy, she could ignore it and get back to him later.

"Happy Monday. How was your day?"

Jeremiah frowned. It was innocuous. Was it lame? But what else was he going to start with? He hit send and set his phone aside to change the channel. Cooking shows were not his thing.

After a few minutes, his phone buzzed.

"OK. Do u have any time l8r this week? I've hot thongs I want to show u."

He snickered and tapped back a reply.

"Um. Might need to translate that?"

"Got. Things. Hang on."

His phone rang.

"Hello?"

"Seriously. Don't text me." Deidre laughed. "Next time, I'm just calling. I keep thinking I'll get the hang of it and quit embarrassing myself."

"You can turn off autocorrect."

"Tried that, it was even worse. I think I'm just not meant to join this century. Anyway, the question stands. Do you have time to swing by this week? I have some things I'd like to show you and see if you have ideas."

"I always have ideas." Lately, the ideas he'd been having where Deidre was concerned fell into a more romantic category than she probably expected. Although, she'd been the one to curl her fingers in his. Jeremiah flipped through his mental schedule. "Wednesday after two?"

"Sure." Deidre took a deep breath, like she was about to speak, but said nothing. Was she still there? "Do you maybe want to stay for dinner?"

His heart leapt. "Yeah, I'd like that. Can I bring something?"

"Want to grab dessert?"

"I can do that."

"Great." She cleared her throat. "Then I guess I'll see you then."

"Okay."

"Okay."

He grinned. "Good night."

Jeremiah hoisted himself onto his mother's kitchen counter and dipped a finger into the batter she was mixing. She smacked his hand and he laughed.

"If you don't behave, I won't send this cake home with you and then what will you take on your date tomorrow night?"

"I could stop at the grocery store and pick something up. But it wouldn't be nearly as good." He snuck another finger swipe from the bowl. "Besides, weren't you the one reminding me about your desire for grandchildren lately?"

"So?"

"So, this can be your contribution to the cause."

She shook her head and folded beaten egg whites into the chocolate mixture. "If you need your grandma's sponge cake to win her heart, I'm not sure she's the one for you."

"Let's just say I'm covering all the bases. Besides, it's not like it can hurt, right?"

Jeremiah's dad sauntered into the kitchen, sniffing. "Do I smell chocolate cake?"

"It's not even in the pan yet. And it's not for you, anyway. I'm making it for Jeremiah to woo Deidre with."

"Deidre? The girl who was over for Sunday dinner two weeks ago? I liked her." He patted Jeremiah's arm. "Why don't you bring her back here for dinner?"

"You just want the cake." Jeremiah grinned.

"Oh, for heaven's sake, I'll make a little cupcake for you, honey. Leave the boy alone. No one wants to go to their parents' house on a date."

"What do you mean? I took you to my parents' house all the time when we were dating. You said you loved it."

"No. I said I loved *you*. It's an important distinction and you're lucky I was willing to make it."

"Hmph. I don't recall you complaining when Mom gave you all her recipes."

Jeremiah's mom smiled. "That's because you have trouble remembering what you ate for breakfast most days."

"Son, let me give you a piece of advice: stay single."

Jeremiah laughed. "Whatever. You'd be lost without Mom. Plus, you got me out of the bargain."

"True enough. You mowing lawns again this summer?"

"Yes, sir. You signing up?"

His dad nodded. "Your mother says I'm too old to be doing my own lawn work. Guess if I have to pay someone it might as well be you, though your rates went up when you got out of high school."

His mom slid the cake pans into the oven and set the timer. "Why don't you take Jeremiah outside and talk to him about that waterfall and pond I want?"

His dad rolled his eyes and jerked his head toward the back door. "Saw it on some TV show and won't let it go. Think that's something you can pull off?"

Jeremiah shrugged. He hadn't done a water feature before, but he'd watched some tutorials online. He could probably figure it out. He hopped down from the counter and kissed his mother's cheek. "Let's go see."

11

Deidre hummed under her breath as she scrubbed the dust and grime from years of neglect off the walls of the front sitting room. It was a beautiful space. Well, it would be once she had it polished up. The wood-paneled walls gleamed in the morning sunlight that streamed in from the nearly floor-to-ceiling windows on the two outside walls. There wasn't much work to be done in here. The ceiling would need some plaster repair, and there were a few pieces missing from the parquet wood floor. But otherwise, it was probably the room that was in the best shape.

A tap at the window made her jolt and slosh soapy water from her bucket onto the floor. She mopped up the spill before turning. Her heart sank. She dropped her scrub brush into the bucket and wiped her hands on her jeans as she strode to the front door. She yanked it open, coming face to face with Paul's cameraman. Paul hovered a few steps away with his toothpaste commercial smile already in place.

"Back up, Greg."

"Hey, D. This is going to be a great project." Greg grinned and shifted, pointing the camera into the front hall.

Deidre stepped out of the house and tugged the door closed behind her. "It is. But it's my project and you won't be a part of it."

"Please. I was hoping you'd take the weekend to read the contracts again and realize just how wrong you are, Deidre. I don't want this to get ugly." Paul's velvety voice oozed onto her nerves. What had she ever seen in him?

"I did actually take another look at them. They still don't apply. See, I'm not flipping this property. And D-Constructs is closing. Our last day in business will be Friday. All the crews have been notified and there's no longer any work underway." Deidre offered a tight smile. "So you can just pack up and go find someone else to hustle."

Paul sighed and fished his cell phone out of the front pocket of his shirt. "Please, you can't possibly believe I'd fall for that, can you? You'd sooner sell your soul than close your business. I didn't want it to come to this, D."

Deidre slid out her own phone and dialed her dad. He answered on the second ring. "Hey, Dad. Could you conference in the company attorney? I don't have her number handy and Paul's on the doorstep with his crew. Again."

Paul pressed a button on his phone and a man's voice crackled through it. "Hello?"

"We're here, Stan, go ahead." Paul smirked.

"Ms. McIntyre, this is Stanfield Barton, the attorney for Flippin' for You and all their interests. I'm aware of the agreements you signed at the time your employment with the show was terminated—"

Terminated? What a lot of gall. She shot Paul a furious glare. She'd left of her own accord and everyone on the crew knew it. "Hold on one moment please, Mr. Barton, my own attorney is on the phone, I can put her on speaker or the two of you can just call one another and talk. I suspect you'll find that Paul has misrepresented the facts of the situation."

Paul shook his head.

"We can certainly take this to a private conversation, but I filed an injunction to have all work on the premises halted until the disagreement has been settled."

"You can't do that." Deidre glared at Paul. "Tell him he can't do that, Ms. Bennigan."

"I'll need to look everything over. Please fax me copies." The attorney rattled of her contact information. "Deidre, even if the injunction holds, that's still private property. If you don't want them there, they're trespassing. You should call the police."

"I'll do that. Thanks." After a promise to get back to her after speaking with Paul's attorney, the lawyer hung up. Deidre crossed her arms. "Leave, Paul."

"I don't think so. I'm sure my attorney will be calling back any minute giving us the green light to begin filming."

Deidre held his gaze for several heartbeats before nodding. Fine. She could play hardball, too. She dialed the police. "Yes, hello, I have trespassers at Peacock Hill who refuse to leave. I've asked nicely several times...yes...thank you. You have about eight minutes, Paul, before you're escorted from the property. And as much as I'd love to see that happen, it couldn't possibly be good for your image. In fact, maybe I should start recording this myself, I'm sure all your fans online would love to see the real you."

He crossed his arms. "I'm well within my rights. I don't believe you aren't flipping this place. Not for one minute. Lisette said you didn't have any plans for it."

"Just because Lisette doesn't believe me, doesn't mean she's right. Six minutes."

Greg lowered the camera from his shoulder. "Maybe...we should go. We can always come back when we get the go-ahead."

"Go sit in the van, if you're that worried." Paul leaned against one of the columns holding the roof of the porch. "She's bluffing."

Before much longer, two police cars, lights flashing, pulled in behind the production van. "Ms. McIntyre?"

Deidre waved. "Thanks for getting here so quickly. Paul and his crew refuse to leave, even though this is private property and they're not welcome."

"Sir, I'm going to have to ask you to get back in your vehicle and vacate the premises." One of the policemen stepped onto the porch, his hand resting on the gun at his hip, and gestured to the van.

Paul shook his head. "I have every right to be here. I'm sure my attorney will be calling back in just a moment to—" He stopped speaking as his phone rang and he pushed the speaker button. "This is Paul."

"Paul, it's Stan. It's best if you go ahead and leave Ms. McIntyre alone. I've sent you an email with more detail, and you can call me with any questions."

Paul's mouth dropped open.

Deidre smirked. "Bye, Paul."

The policeman gave a grim smile and gestured again to the van.

Paul made his way down the steps, shaking his head.

Deidre waited until Paul was on his way down the driveway before smiling at the police. "Thanks again."

They waved and followed Paul, their lights still on for as long as she could see them. Letting out a big breath, she called her Dad back.

"Hey, Dad. Thanks for that."

"It's no problem, hon. Claire says all the crews are set up with their regulars. No one really even complained. I think what you're doing is a brave thing, in case you wondered."

Deidre sank down on the steps and leaned against a pillar. "Is it? You're not upset?"

"Not at all. I'd planned to close down when I retired, you know that. When you took it over, made it something amazing, I was proud as can be. But it's been clear to me your heart hasn't been in it since Paul got you kicked off the show."

She bristled. Did everyone think that? "I wasn't kicked off, Dad. I left. Voluntarily."

"Because you knew they'd kick you off if you didn't. There's no shame in that. Just like there's no shame in finding something new you love to do. From the pictures you sent your mom and me, that place down there is going to be magnificent."

It really was. But... "Do you honestly think I can do it? What do I know about weddings and events?"

"So you'll figure it out. You know how to run a business and to hire people who are good at their jobs. Seems to me, between that and your willingness to learn, you'll be just fine. What are you really afraid of?"

So many things. "How do I know this is the right decision?"

"You've been praying about it, right?"

Her heart sank. "Not until recently."

"Mmm. Better late than never. Pray. Listen. And see what God works out. From where I'm sitting, it seems pretty clear that God has His hand on this."

Things had definitely been going smoothly—basically from the start. "Okay. Thanks, Dad."

"I love you, honey. Your mom and I are praying for you, too."

She ended the call and stared over the front lawn that merged into a forested hill that led down to the main road. *God? I'm sorry I haven't been talking this all over with You. I was mad...at Paul and maybe a little at You. I always thought that TV show was going to be for me...and when it turned out it wasn't...I got so mad. I'm sorry. I want to do what You want me to do. Will You show me what that is? Please?*

Deidre tossed a sheet over the folding table she'd picked up on a quick run into town for groceries the other day and glanced around the parlor. Besides the few remaining cosmetic repairs needed, this room was ready to be marked off her to-do list. Which made it the best place to have dinner with someone who could make her whole body warm with just a look. Did he have any idea what he did to her? She blew out a breath. Was she ready to go there again? Paul's betrayal had stung, and the repercussions had been enormous. But without that, would she ever have admitted, even to herself, that D-

Constructs wasn't her dream? That she was simply marking time and doing what she thought was expected?

Dad never expected it. He'd confirmed that—again—this morning on the phone. Still, she didn't regret the years she'd invested into that business, or the skills she'd learned. She loved the process of fixing up and rehabbing buildings. But she yearned for the chance to be a part of what happened next. Peacock Hill was going to give her that.

She dug her phone out of her pocket and checked the time. Nearly two. Jeremiah could show up any time. She should've pressed for something more concrete so she wouldn't have the grasshopper rodeo that was currently taking place in her stomach. Or maybe she would. She'd held his hand on Saturday. He hadn't seemed to mind. The fact of the matter was she couldn't have let go if she wanted to. And she hadn't wanted to. Jeremiah made her think in terms of forever.

Movement out the window caught her eye. She turned and watched as Jeremiah parked his truck and got out, holding a bouquet of deep pink flowers and what looked like a cake. He bumped the door with his hip so it closed and took the steps to the porch in long strides. Her heart gave a lazy flip.

His knock jolted her out of her thoughts and she hurried to the door. She pulled it open and the sight of him made her stop and catch her breath. "Right on time."

Jeremiah's eyes sparkled with laughter as he held out the roses. "These are for you."

Deidre buried her nose in the blooms and peeked up at him through her lashes. "Thanks. Come on in. Why don't we head to the kitchen and you can put that down and I can get these some water?"

"Sure." He scanned the area. "You've been cleaning."

She nodded as she crossed the length of the wide foyer to the kitchen at the back of the house. "No sense in starting work if you've got a layer of grime."

"I haven't seen the kitchen. It's...kitschy. I like it."

"I do, too. And everything still works. I don't think I'll do much in here. Maybe a few little tweaks since I'll want it to work as a semi-commercial kitchen, but if I can avoid the stainless take over, I will." She nodded to the long island that ran the length of the space. "You can set that anywhere."

Jeremiah set down the cake and tucked his hands in his pockets. "You won't have room for a big kitchen staff."

Deidre levered herself onto the counter and rose to her knees so she could reach the top shelf of the cupboard where she'd stored the glass vase she'd unearthed when cleaning out one of the rooms on the third floor. Normally, she didn't bother with shelves up that high—but she hadn't expected to ever need it. It was a simple thing, probably came from the florist with a delivery, but it saved her the humiliation of using a pitcher for the flowers. "I don't think we'll need one. The kinds of events I'm thinking we'll be used for are smaller, more intimate. Or they'll be catered from outside and just use the kitchen for setup."

She turned. Jeremiah stood directly in front of her. He reached for the vase. "Can I help you with that?"

Her heart hammered in her chest. "I have it."

Still, her grip loosened as he took the container and set it on the counter. He brushed the back of his fingers across her cheek, his other hand coming to rest on her hip. Her gaze locked with his as he leaned forward slowly. She could say something. Evade. Her tongue darted between her lips. She didn't want to.

Jeremiah's lips brushed hers, a feather-light touch that sent shivers through her. Deidre shifted, her eyes drifting closed as her hands found his shoulders and their lips met again.

He eased back, a smile hovering at the corner of his mouth. "Hi."

"Hi, yourself. I guess we skipped that earlier." She pressed her lips together and twisted a tiny bit. Her knees were beginning to protest the time she was spending on the counter. "I like this version though."

"Me, too. Can I help you down?" Jeremiah grinned and offered her a hand. Taking it, she shifted and hopped to the floor. He tugged, pulling her close and wrapping her in his arms, his lips brushing hers again.

Deidre tried to rein in her scattered thoughts. "Water. For the roses. I should get them in water."

Neither one of them moved. After a moment, Deidre sighed and rested her head against his chest. She could stay like this forever. His chuckle was a quiet rumble under her ear. He gave her a nudge, his arms loosening. "Get the water. I'll go back around the other side of the island or we'll never get to those things you wanted to show me."

"Right. To see if you had ideas."

He winked. "I think I've already shown you the best ideas I've been having lately."

Her cheeks heated and she held the vase under the faucet and fumbled with the taps. "You're not going to get any complaints from me."

12

Jeremiah whistled as he unloaded his tools from the back of his truck. It had taken longer than he'd anticipated to get the materials he needed for the stone work at Peacock Hill, but now they were here and he'd cleared all his current jobs so he could dedicate a week, at least, to getting it done. A week of seeing Deidre every day. Not that they hadn't both made excuses to find an hour here or there since Wednesday, but it wasn't quite the same. Nothing was the same in the last almost-week.

Deidre opened the front door and he grinned as his heart leapt. Would he always have this response, or was it just the newness of their relationship? It was different than it had been with Elise. He thanked God every morning for that.

"I brought you some coffee. Thought you might want some before you get started." Barefoot, she came down the steps, two steaming mugs in her hands.

"I never say no to coffee." He took the mug and drank. He didn't need the caffeine with her around, but it was coffee.

"They delivered the stone yesterday. I had them leave it around the side, since that's where most of the work is needed. There's a wheelbarrow over there too, so you can cart what you need for the steps." Deidre turned and eyed the front of the house.

"I thought I'd start in the front, unless you have deliveries or something coming that'll need to use that entrance?"

She shook her head. "That's fine. I'm not expecting anyone."

He turned and set his mug on the truck before drawing her into his arms and lowering his lips to hers. "Good morning."

"Morning. You're cheerful." She wiggled out of his embrace but slipped one arm around his waist.

"It's your fault."

She chuckled. "I suppose I can live with that. The weather's supposed to hold all week, so that's nice. They're saying rain next week though."

"We'll play it by ear. I should be able to get a good bit of it done before it's an issue. You've made incredible progress in the month you've been here." He rubbed her arm before turning to collect his coffee. "It's nice to see the old girl perking up."

"It really is. My sister's moving down next week to help once she gets all the final details of closing D-Constructs taken care of."

"How are you doing with that?" Jeremiah turned to study her expression. She didn't have the pale, hollow-eyed appearance of someone who spent their evenings crying. But maybe that wasn't her way.

"Surprisingly well. It was time." Deidre nodded, as if reassuring herself. "I've had emails from a few of the guys on various crews; they're still getting plenty of work. That was my major concern, that we'd be putting them out of business too. But in the end, I'm not sure we were ever really necessary."

"Sure you were. It's hard to start a handyman business from the ground up. I can attest to that. So can your dad. You gave them a start. People didn't have to worry, as much, about references and guarantees, because you were a known name. Now, even though you're gone, they have enough business in the background to make it on their own. That's an amazing thing you gave them. You should be proud of it."

Slowly, Deidre nodded. "Thanks. It's hard, not being able to see how all the pieces are going to fit together. When I took over from Dad, even though I changed the name and altered the business model a little, I knew how everything worked and what I needed to do to make it a success. I had control. This...is marginally terrifying."

"Only marginally?" Jeremiah winked.

She elbowed his side.

"I think this is good for you. It's a chance to fully rely on God, because you don't have any other choice."

She sighed. "That's a tall order. Mom and Dad always said God gave us brains, so we were to use them."

"I don't disagree. But using your brain, doing what you think is right and makes sense, doesn't preclude relying on God. It's not an either-or proposition. I don't think God asks us to sit on our hands and wait for a divine nudge before we get dressed in the morning."

"That's not what I meant."

"I know, but the idea's the same. If your intent is to do what God wants for you, if that's what you're praying for and earnestly seeking, then you start on the path that makes sense and listen. God's pretty good about making it clear when you need to turn."

"Maybe for you."

"I don't know. From what you told me about Flippin' for You, it seems like God made it clear it wasn't where He wanted you."

She scoffed. "In a blaze of fire."

"Well." He hesitated, not sure if he should ask but unable to bite back the words. "Were there little things before then, maybe from the very start that could have kept you from that path if you'd been listening to them?"

Deidre pulled her lower lip between her teeth. After a moment, she gave a small nod. "Yeah. I guess, looking back, there were. So...what? I'm just horrible at hearing God?"

He chuckled and pulled her closer to his side. "That's not what I'm saying. I'm not perfect at it, either. But it gets easier, the more you do it. When things come up, you stop and pray and see if you get clearer direction."

"Okay. So...Paul coming here, causing problems? What's that?"

Jeremiah rubbed the back of his neck. "I want easy answers, too. I think we all do. The fact is, I don't know. Sometimes I think you have to weigh the good against the bad. And never stop praying. But didn't you say you think that issue's resolved?"

"Yeah."

He kissed her forehead. "Then I think you just keep moving forward, praying and listening as you go."

"All right. You'll pray with me?"

"Absolutely."

"Why aren't you hanging out with Deidre tonight?" Danny flopped onto Jeremiah's couch and toed off his shoes. "Not that I'm complaining."

"She needed to head back north and help her sister pack. I got the feeling she wanted to see her folks and brother, too." Jeremiah shrugged. He'd half expected she might ask him to come along. He'd almost volunteered. But...maybe it was too soon. Though she'd met his parents.

"What?"

"What what?"

"You look pensive."

Jeremiah shook his head. "It's nothing. When do you think Matt'll get here?"

"After the garage closes, I imagine. You in a rush?"

"No. Sorry. I'm just...wired, I guess."

Danny snorted. "You've got it bad, man."

Jeremiah shrugged again. "Are we doing pizza or am I throwing something on the grill?"

"Your house, your call. What are you in the mood for?" The doorbell rang and Danny pointed toward the hall. "That's probably Matt. Why don't you ask him?"

"Ask me what?" Matt kicked his shoes into the corner and dropped into the recliner. "Figured the doorbell let you know I was friendly. You order the pizza yet?"

"We were just discussing pizza versus grilling." Jeremiah stuck his hands in his pockets. "You want pizza?"

Matt shook his head. "Not necessarily, it's just what we always do, so I kind of figured. But if you want to grill, I'm game. Whatcha got?"

"Burgers?"

"I like burgers." Danny smiled. "Especially burgers I don't have to make."

"Sure, I'm game. What's the deal with all the domesticity?"

Danny's voice took on a sing-song quality. "He's in looooove."

"Yeah? With the new girl, what's her name, Denise?"

Jeremiah frowned. What was so hard about her name that people couldn't remember it? "Deidre. And I didn't say that. We just started hanging out. I'm not even sure you can call it dating. It's not like we're going out all the time."

Matt nodded at Danny. "Nailed it in one, didn't you? Listen to him hedge."

"I'm not hedging. You two are idiots. I'm going to go turn on the grill." Jeremiah stalked out of the living room and into the kitchen. He paused to call back over his shoulder, "You know where the drinks are if you want something."

Stepping out onto the deck, he pulled the cover off the grill and opened the lid. In love. He couldn't be in love with Deidre. Could he? No. There was no possible way. He'd known her a month. He liked her. A lot. And he could see how it might turn into something more down the road, but time was key. He'd jumped into those words with Elise and he wasn't making that mistake again. The next time he told a woman he loved her, he was going to be sure she really meant it when she said it back.

Back in the kitchen, he got ground beef out of the fridge and dumped it in a bowl, cracking an egg over it and squirting a healthy dollop of steak sauce in for good measure. He ground salt and pepper over it and reached in, squishing it together with his hands. When it was mixed, he formed three gigantic patties and set them on a plate.

"Need any help?" Matt ambled into the kitchen and leaned against the island.

"Nope. We're set. How's everything at the garage?"

Matt lifted a shoulder. "Same old. Though we've got a few folks from Waynesboro coming over to us, which is nice. Mr. Patterson was starting to wonder if he'd need to close up shop."

"You talk to him about buying him out yet?"

"Not yet."

"Why not?" Jeremiah washed his hands and picked up the plate with the burgers, jerking his head toward the deck. "If he's thinking of closing up, shouldn't you let him know you're interested in carrying on?"

"What if it's not viable? I figure we probably do routine maintenance on eighty percent of the population, but they're going outside for major repairs. Oil changes aren't really a sustainable business model in a small town." Matt hooked his thumbs in his back pockets and followed Jeremiah onto the deck.

Jeremiah laid the burgers on the grill, smiling as they sizzled. "Mr. Patterson's managed for what, forty years? How much of wanting to close up is a desire to retire? You need to talk to him, man."

"Yeah, I guess. So, Danny right? You in love?"

Jeremiah shook his head. "Not yet."

Matt considered a moment and nodded. "You want to be."

"Let's just say I see possibilities and leave it at that."

13

"I'm so glad you're home." Deidre's mom wrapped her in a tight hug and kissed the top of her head. "Even if you're only here for the weekend. The house has been quiet without you."

Deidre shook her head. "You know you're enjoying it. Weren't you on my case about finding a roommate, getting an apartment just three months ago?"

"Well, yes. But I didn't expect you to move three hours away. I like having you nearby."

"Yeah, well, they don't have Peacock Hill nearby. It's where I'm supposed to be, Mom." Deidre squeezed her mom's hand and dropped into a seat at the breakfast table. She'd gotten in last night, basically just in time to get to bed after saying hello. It was good to be home. "Dad back in the den?"

"Of course. Watching some home improvement show or other. I'm not sure why he retired when all he does is tinker in the workshop or watch those shows. Why not just keep doing?"

"This way he gets to hang out with you more. You know you love it. Besides, I thought you had a list of improvements you wanted to do around here? Get him started on those." Deidre stood and crossed the room to poke her head in the den. "Morning, Dad."

"D! You're up." He clicked the TV off and stood, holding out his arms. "I'm so glad you came home for the weekend. Bring any pictures of your progress?"

She chuckled. "On my phone. Sit down. You might even like some of these, Mom. There's this really gorgeous tromp l'oeil in the breakfast room that I think you'll love. I'm going to try to keep it from getting damaged, but the plaster needs a lot of work, so I'm not sure if I'll succeed."

Her dad sat on the sofa next to her and, after a moment's hesitation, her mom sat on the other side. Deidre smiled and thumbed to her photos. Her mom tried to stay out of the handyman and renovation talk. Something about wanting her daughter to have a special connection with her dad. But Deidre had never really understood it. Why couldn't her mom just embrace what her daughter loved, even if it was something she shared with her dad, too? Either way, they'd found a tentative common ground with decorating and Deidre was doing whatever she could to capitalize on it. "Here we are. See, Mom?"

Her mother angled her head and nodded. "Those leaves are so lifelike. And the birds...I hope you can work around it, but that water damage is really close, isn't it?"

Deidre nodded and scrolled to the next photo that had another close up of the art, this time with a huge crack running through it. "I don't think I can do anything about this one."

"What if you documented it carefully and then did what you needed to do to fix it and found someone to re-create the paintings when you were finished?" Dad reached over to the phone and flipped to the next photo.

"Oh. Well now. Who's that?" Her mother's voice warmed with approval.

Heat crawled up Deidre's neck and she cleared her throat. "That's Jeremiah. He's doing the stone work."

"Mmmhmm." Her mother arched an eyebrow. "Married?"

"No." Deidre flipped to the next photo. Unfortunately, it also featured Jeremiah. How many pictures had she snapped of him while he'd been busy working? Clearly she'd been enjoying the view a bit too much.

"Looks like he does good work. Keep going." Her father's voice was less amused than her mom's.

Deidre scrolled as quickly as she could past the pictures with anyone other than the house in them. "Here's the new roof I put on."

"Oh, go back. I want to know more about this young man. He's quite handsome. Seems to know his way around tools. And...he's captured your interest. Which makes him interesting to me." Deidre's mom patted her knee. "Do you only see him on the job site?"

"I've been going to church with him, too."

"Really?" Her father nodded. "Maybe he's not so bad after all. Why haven't you mentioned him?"

"Because I didn't want the Spanish Inquisition?"

"Darn it, I broke the rack down for parts just last week. What did you do with those manacles, dear?" Her dad sent her mother a bland stare.

"Didn't you use them as planters?"

"Fine. You two are ridiculous. We're...dating. I guess."

Her father frowned. "Shouldn't you know if you're dating someone or not?"

Deidre hunched her shoulders. "We haven't really talked about it."

"So what makes you think you're dating and not, say, good friends?" Her mother's stare was like a laser boring into her soul.

Flames licked at every nerve ending. This was exactly why she hadn't wanted to mention him. She'd wanted to wait until she knew what was going on. But she also didn't need to be the one to bring up the conversation with Jeremiah. Pushing Paul had been the first step toward the end. "We might have kissed."

Her mother made a humming sound as her father pushed to his feet.

"Dad. I'm twenty-six. You realize I've kissed people before."

Her mother laid her hand on her arm and made a tsking sound. "That's not going to help, Deidre. Honey, sit down."

Her father sat, arms crossed, and glared at Deidre a moment before shaking his head. "How do you kiss someone if you don't know whether or not you're dating? Is this what the world has come to? No wonder people don't bother getting married any more. They just shack up because no one can be bothered to make any kind of relationship status official. After all, someone better might come along, so why commit?"

"Dad. It's not like that." Was it? She'd never seen him with another girl. He'd never mentioned one. And there was no one at church giving them the evil eye...surely if he had someone else, she would've made her presence known. "It's just...new, okay?"

"New. Old enough to be kissing, but still new enough that you don't know what it is." Her father waved his hand, cutting her off before she could speak. "I know, I know, it's different now. Show me the rest of the house. Then you need to use that thing for its intended purpose and ask this young man what his plans are before I do it for you."

Deidre winced and flipped to the next photo on her phone. He would, too. That wasn't a question. This was the man who'd called her prom date's parents when the guy was fifteen minutes late picking her up because he'd had a flat tire. That had been an awesome way to start the evening. "I love you, Dad."

"I know that. And I love you, too. But you're not getting around me that way this time." He winked and patted her knee.

Deidre paced the length of her parents' small suburban back yard and stared at her phone. She couldn't go inside without a definitive answer. And she couldn't bring herself to call him. He'd surely laugh. Or worse. What if this messed everything up? She *liked* Jeremiah. A lot. She wanted him around for a long time to come. She closed her eyes and stopped in her tracks. Was she falling in love with him?

Swallowing the nerves that wanted to crawl up her throat, she tapped her phone. Call or text? It'd be easier to get it out in writing without sounding like a fool. She'd just double check every letter before she hit send. Three times. She tapped out a message.

"Random ? 4u – r we serrated?"

No. She stared at the phone. Serious. How did it get serrated out of serious? And now he was going to think she was an even bigger dork than he probably already did.

"I do think you're sharp – intellectually speaking. And a snappy dresser to boot."

Ding-a-ling. She couldn't stop a smile though as she tapped back.

"Dating. Are we?"

There. No mistakes. And she looked like a needy and obsessive teenager who had to shoehorn a guy into a relationship definition conversation at the first possible opportunity. Why wasn't he answering? Gah. She was twenty-six years old. She didn't need to do stuff like this just because her dad told her to. So why had she? Because she wanted to know the answer.

Insecure.

Wasn't that what Paul had yelled at her as part of his tirade three weeks before it became clear she wasn't wanted on the show anymore? And now she'd proven it. Again.

He wasn't texting back. She slid her phone in her back pocket and trudged to the house.

"Well?" Her dad glanced up from the kitchen table.

Deidre shrugged. "He didn't answer. So I guess not. Happy?"

"It's Saturday morning, maybe he's on a job and can't get to his phone. Give him some time." Her dad patted her arm as she walked past. Sure. That's why he'd responded the first time. There was no point in getting into it with her dad. He was a great dad, but not really the person you went to when you heart was breaking. "Your brother and sister should be here any minute. Why don't we plan to go to that restaurant where they bring meat around on skewers for dinner?"

"Yeah. Sure." Not even the prospect of seeing Duncan and eating at a churrascaria could lift her heart out of her shoes. She dragged herself up the stairs to her room and sat on the bed. How pathetic was it that, at twenty-six, she was still more at home in her old bedroom than anywhere else? Deidre took a deep breath and gave herself a firm mental shake. She was going to make a success out of Peacock Hill. Even if she had to do it with a broken heart.

14

Jeremiah checked the map on his phone. Fifteen minutes to go a mile? How did people live up here? It was Saturday evening. Didn't these people have places to be? He crept forward as the traffic on the D.C. Beltway inched ahead. At this rate, he wasn't going to be there until well after Deidre and her family were seated. Would Claire be able to save him a seat? Did it matter?

For the six millionth time, he questioned his decision not to text back. But some things just needed to be done in person. Claire, at least, seemed to think he was doing the right thing. Hopefully, Deidre's sister knew her well enough to know if this was right or horribly wrong.

His phone rang. Jeremiah punched the speaker button. "Yeah?"

"Hey man, you there yet?"

Danny. He'd laughed for a good five minutes when Jeremiah had called to ask if he'd gotten Claire's number. Of course, he'd had to explain the whole situation. But his friend had come through with the contact info so... "Not yet. The traffic up here is insane. I thought Charlottesville at rush hour was bad."

Danny scoffed. "I keep telling you, man. C-ville's nothing. It's why I don't really mind the commute. Let me know how it goes, okay? And say hi to Claire for me."

"Sure. Will do."

"I'll be praying."

"Appreciate it." Jeremiah disconnected the call and banged on his steering wheel. If he had to drive up here with any regularity he'd go insane. Finally, there was a gap big enough to squeak his truck over into the exit lane. He gunned the engine. Maybe it was a pointless exercise, but it felt good after creeping along. He might actually make it before dessert after all.

The phone directed him through the maze of office buildings that made up Tyson's Corner and, after another almost ten minutes, he pulled up to the valet stand outside the restaurant. He grabbed his blazer off the passenger seat, tucked his phone into the pocket of his khakis, and smoothed the pink and black striped tie his mother insisted matched the cobalt blue dress shirt. After taking a ticket from a kid who appeared entirely too young to be parking cars, he took a deep breath and shrugged into the coat. If the reflection in the glass doors was any indication, he at least looked presentable.

Jeremiah swallowed and reached for the handle.

Inside, the quiet rumble of conversation melded with the clinking of glasses and silverware. The hostess smiled from behind her podium. "May I help you?"

"Hi. Um, McIntyre?" Jeremiah's hands were clammy and he fought the urge to wipe them on his pants.

"Of course. The rest of your party is already seated. Right this way." She slipped from behind the podium and glided through a doorway into the main restaurant.

Jeremiah followed behind her, eyes scanning the tables. There she was. He couldn't help the grin. Everything about her shone like a beacon in the night.

The hostess stopped at the table and, with another smile, headed back toward the front of the restaurant.

Jeremiah cleared his throat as Deidre glanced up and met his gaze. "Hi."

"Jeremiah." Deidre half stood, then settled back into her chair, her expression cooling. "What brings you here?"

He licked his lips. Out of the corner of his eye, he caught Claire's encouraging nod. "I got your text, but I thought it seemed like something we ought to talk about in person."

Deidre's father stood and offered his hand. "Since my daughter seems to have misplaced her manners, you must be Jeremiah."

"Yes, sir. It's a pleasure to meet you." Jeremiah shook his hand and managed a weak smile for Deidre's mother. "Ma'am."

"Have a seat, won't you?" Deidre's mother pointed to the empty chair next to Deidre. "They should be bringing the meat around soon. I hope you'll join us."

"I'd like that very much. Thank you." He pulled out the chair and, as he sat, leaned close to Deidre and whispered, "To answer your question from this morning, I very much hope so."

She blinked and turned toward him, mouth slightly open.

How he wanted to lean in just a little more and kiss her. But her father was watching with eagle-eyed interest. As was the rest of her family. So he simply smiled, took the napkin from the center of his plate, and spread it over his lap.

"So, Jeremiah, what brings you up this way? You live down near Peacock Hill, don't you?"

"Yes, ma'am, I do. I actually came up because Deidre texted me this morning, so I called Claire and she suggested that I join you for supper."

Deidre's mouth dropped open again. "Claire?"

Claire smiled. "Duncan knew too."

Duncan lifted his water glass and toasted Jeremiah from across the table. "Nice to meet you. I've heard a lot of good things."

Had he? From whom? It didn't seem like Deidre had been talking him up to her parents. So, Claire? "Thanks. Likewise."

Duncan chuckled. "If I know Dee, all she said was that I'm a landscaper."

She hadn't even really said that much. Just that her brother loved his job in D.C. but that things weren't going so well. Jeremiah shrugged. "Something like that."

"Yeah, well, I think it's the nature of little sisters. At least mine. They don't want me to get a big head." Duncan sipped his water.

"What did Deidre text you about?" Her dad crossed his arms in front of him on the table.

"Well, sir, Deidre and I just started dating. But our relationship is new enough, we hadn't really sat down and defined it. That's my fault. I didn't make my intentions clear." Jeremiah shifted and caught Deidre's eye. "I'm sorry. I would very much like to date you. Exclusively. I have feelings for you. And I hope you feel the same."

Pink stole across her cheeks as Deidre nodded.

"That wasn't so hard, was it?" Deidre's father shook his head and mumbled what sounded like "young people these days."

Jeremiah smothered a smile and reached for Deidre's hand.

She curled her fingers through his. "I'm glad you came."

"Me, too."

Deidre nestled against Jeremiah's shoulder as they sat on the gliding rocker on the patio behind Deidre's parents' house. It was just about perfect. A lovely spring evening with his girl by his side.

"I'm glad you came up. I should've called instead of texting though. I really don't know why I try."

He smiled and pressed a kiss to the top of her head. "I think it's cute."

She made a rude noise. "Sure. Just wait 'til it gets really embarrassing."

"No group texts. Then it won't matter."

"That's a deal." She sighed and shifted. "I could stay like this forever."

Forever. It's what he wanted too, despite being entirely too soon to be thinking that way. "Why don't we work on making that happen?"

"Really?" Her eyes filled with hope.

"Really." He wrapped his arm around her, drew her close, and lowered his mouth to hers, sealing their future with a kiss.

Want a Free Book?

If you enjoyed A Heart Restored and would like to read one of my full-length novels for free, you can get a free ebook simply by signing up for my newsletter here: http://bit.ly/2g0AGvf

Turn the page for a sneak peek at *A Heart Reclaimed, Peacock Hill Romance Book Two*

Chapter 1

Anna Hamilton parked her car under one of the shaggy cedars near the front of Peacock Hill and rubbed her hands together. Finally, a chance to be part of a project that mattered. Not that the historical landscape archives weren't important, but who wanted to be stuck behind a desk helping researchers when she could get her hands in the dirt? She couldn't really pinpoint how she'd ended up at the library, either. Which just made it worse. But now...maybe her life was back on track.

Gathering her laptop bag and her duffel, she stepped out of the car and breathed in the unpolluted air. It was lovely. Very little humidity and still cooler than Richmond, which was beginning to feel the first tendrils of Virginia summer weather. Even if it was barely May. She closed the car door and crossed the gravel drive, climbing the steps to the front of the house two at a time while she admired the columns and general grandeur of the place.

Anna knocked on the door. Would anyone hear if they weren't close by? The house—there had to be a better word. Mansion? Estate?—was massive.

"Coming." Footsteps clomped closer before the door swung open. The tiny blonde grinned and extended her hand. "Anna, right? I'm Deidre."

"That's me. Nice to meet you." Anna took her hand and peered inside. Rich wood—on the floor and the walls—met her gaze. "Gosh, it's even prettier in real life."

"Come on in. Is that all you brought?"

"I have more out in the car—you said to be prepared to rough it, so there's an air mattress and that kind of thing, too. I just wasn't sure..."

Deidre grinned. "I've got an actual mattress for you. It's on the floor, but it's better than a blow up. We're roughing it, but not quite at the camping level. You and I are on the second floor. I stuck my brother on the third."

"Sounds good."

Deidre paused and angled her head to the side.

Anna raised her brows. "What?"

"It's just...I want to make sure you didn't think you were in charge of the project?"

Anna worked to control the expression on her face. She *had* actually, but diplomacy was always a good idea. "Well, you have final say, of course."

Deidre shook her head. "I was afraid of that. I'm so sorry. See, my brother's a landscape architect and I asked him—practically as soon as I bought the place—to help out. I wasn't sure he'd be able to get down here this spring though, which is why I started looking around for photos and such—to see if I could do a little cleanup while I waited for him to have time. But his work schedule cleared up and he got here yesterday."

"I see." Although she didn't. Anna gripped the handle of her duffel. Three months of email and phone calls with Deidre had made her seem like a friend, of sort. Why had the woman never mentioned a brother? A landscaping brother at that. "So...you don't actually need me?"

"I didn't say that. I...it's just..." Deidre broke off and turned at the noise on the staircase.

"Hey, Dee, I was thinking...oh." A tall, sandy-haired man stopped on the steps, his features sliding into a blank mask. "Hello, Anna."

"McIntyre. Of course." Anna's stomach twisted into an entire batch of pretzels as she realized just who Deidre's brother was. She swallowed, willing some moisture into the desert of her mouth. "I should be going. Your project is in good hands."

Deidre shot Duncan a meaningful look.

Anna turned and reached for the door.

"I never figured you for one who'd walk away from a challenge."

Anna spun, scowling, as Duncan crossed the foyer. "You'd dare?"

"I'll just leave the two of you to work this out." Deidre patted Duncan's arm and beat a hasty retreat up the stairs.

"It's good to see you." He tucked his hands into his pockets with a cocky smile. "What's it been, ten years?"

Anna sucked a breath through her teeth. Up close it was clear none of her prayers had been answered since Duncan wasn't balding, pockmarked, or obese. Preferably all three. He was even better looking than he'd been in college, if that was possible. The lanky young man had filled out—in all the right places—and what had been an attractive package was now deadly. "Something like that, yes. Look. I didn't realize she was your sister or I never would've come. Obviously you're more than capable of handling the gardens here after working at Marshall Brothers. I'm surprised they'd let you take the spring off."

He shrugged. "It's more of a leave of absence, to be honest."

"What? You have too many awards to fit in your office, so they sent you away while they built you a new one?" Not that she'd been following his career. Much. He just happened to get written up in all the magazines she enjoyed reading. Needed to read for professional development.

"Not quite." He sighed. "There's been some turnover at the top and I'm not sure I like the new direction they're heading. So, I took some time. Besides, this place? Who wouldn't want to work on it?"

Anna grinned before she could stop it. That was her thought, exactly. "Yes, well. You won this one, too. I'll let you get to it."

"Anna." His voice was quiet. Almost tender. A lot like it had been the last time she'd told him goodbye.

She blinked back the tears that filled her eyes. "What?"

"You're welcome to stay. I could use the help."

Her heart lifted, but she fought it. Trusting Duncan was as risky as planting in mid-January. "What's the catch?"

"Nothing, really. Except that I'm in charge."

Author's Note

Thank you for reading Cookies & Candlelight! I hope that you enjoyed it! I would appreciate it if you'd help others enjoy it too by leaving a review! Word of mouth is how most people say they find new books to read, so I'd love it if you'd also consider telling your friends about it. Any success my books have is owed to readers like you who take the time to tell others about my stories. Thank you, from the bottom of my heart.

Working on this project, with the five other amazing authors who are all writing in Arcadia Valley, has been an absolute delight. I love all the characters who fill up our little town, and I hope you will, too. Each of the ladies who are a part of Arcadia Valley has a great talent and a deep love for Christian fiction. I think you'll agree it shows in the work they produce.

You can always keep up to date with my writing news via my newsletter. There's a sign-up form at my website http://bit.ly/2g0AGvf and also on my author Facebook page

http://www.Facebook.com/ElizabethMaddrey.

I continue to owe a huge debt of gratitude to my husband and sons for giving me the time to write, my sister for her unflinching support and encouragement, and my critique partners Valerie Comer, Lynellen Perry, Heather Gray and Jan Elder for catching all the times I use the same word six times in two paragraphs.

More than anything, I'm grateful that God continues to give me words and makes it possible for me to write them down.

I'd love to hear from you! You can connect with me on Facebook my webpage or via email.

About the Author

Elizabeth Maddrey began writing stories as soon as she could form the letters properly and has never looked back. Though her practical nature and love of computers, math, and organization steered her into computer science at Wheaton College, she always had one or more stories in progress to occupy her free time. This continued through a Master's program in Software Engineering, several years in the computer industry, teaching programming at the college level, and a Ph.D. in Computer Technology in Education. When she isn't writing, Elizabeth is a voracious consumer of books and has mastered the art of reading while undertaking just about any other activity.

Elizabeth is the author of more than ten books, both fiction and non-fiction. She lives in the suburbs of Washington, D.C. with her husband and their two incredibly active little boys.

www.ingramcontent.com/pod-product-compliance
Lightning Source LLC
Chambersburg PA
CBHW022023170626
46808CB00003B/1032